★ 'Praise for

'Fabulous fairies and fashion-forward witches'
Guardian, Best New Children's Books, Summer 2015

'I'm a big fan of the main fairy'
Fran the Fabulous Fairy

'Cheese water – that is so disgusting!'
RTÉJr's The Word

'Fizzing with fun'
Daily Mail

'The craziest and funniest book I've read in ages'
Andy Stanton, author of the Mr Gum *series*

'This book could do with more jam …'
Mavis, owner of Jam Stall No. 9

'The best young fiction I've read in yonks.
Proper grin-worthy'
Phil Earle, author

'I couldn't put this book down and will recommend it to all my friends'
Evie, age 8, for lovereading4kids.co.uk

'Brilliantly written book and fab drawings'
Caitlin, age 7, for lovereading4kids.co.uk

'Yawn. Tiga's adventures are so rubbish'
Felicity Bat, evil witch

'The illustrations are outstanding … I loved this book so much that I would like to read the next book in the series'
Isabella, age 8, for lovereading4kids.co.uk

'I would give it 5 stars'
Ella, age 8, for lovereading4kids.co.uk

'Silly spells, delectable dresses, magical mishaps and ridiculous riddles, this is a witch story like no other – and it's a blast!'
Bookseller

'Fun, friendship, fabulous illustrations'
Parents in Touch

'A completely fresh and fun take on witches,
Witch Wars is for anyone who likes magic, adventure,
fashion or a fabulous story'
Booktrust

'Sibéal Pounder's imagination is boundless – there is
something new and hilarious on every page.
We can't wait for the next one!'
Ruth Fitzgerald, author

'I only review cheese'
Miss Heks, evil guardian

'Bonkers in all the best possible ways, *Witch Wars*
is funny, fabulous and above all a truly great story.
You'll never look at witches the same way after
reading this one'
Katy Cannon, author

'Enchanting characters, witty writing and the best
frocks EVER! This book is a must-have. Original,
funny, with a lovely light touch. I loved it'
Sam Hay, author

Books by Sibéal Pounder

Witch Wars

Witch Switch

Witch Watch

Witch Glitch

WITCH
WATCH

WITCH WATCH

SIBÉAL POUNDER

Illustrated by
Laura Ellen
Anderson

BLOOMSBURY
LONDON OXFORD NEW YORK NEW DELHI SYDNEY

Bloomsbury Publishing, London, Oxford, New York, New Delhi and Sydney

First published in Great Britain in March 2016 by Bloomsbury Publishing Plc
50 Bedford Square, London WC1B 3DP

www.bloomsbury.com

ISBN 978 1 4088 5269 9

Typeset by RefineCatch Limited, Bungay, Suffolk
Printed and bound in Great Britain by CPI Group (UK) Ltd, Croydon CR0 4YY

5 7 9 10 8 6 4

For George and Derrick – S.P.
For Georgia – L.E.A.

THE DOCKS

DESPERATE
DOLLS

DRIPTOWN

THE LAKES

SILVER
CITY

LINDEN HOUSE

RITZY
CITY

Clutterbucks

CAKES, PIES &
'THAT'S ABOUT
IT' REALLY

RITZY CITY

GULL & CHIP
TAVERN

JAM
& CO

The Story So Far

Last time in Ritzy City:

Well, Felicity Bat and Aggie Hoof turned Peggy into a doll, took over Linden House and started undoing all her good work and making the place awful and evil.

Luckily Tiga and Fluffanora figured out what they were doing and – with a little help from Fran the Fabulous Fairy – foiled their plans and saved Peggy. They even saved some other witches too, like the fashion explorer Eddy Eggby, who had been turned into a doll by Celia Crayfish AGES ago and had been stuck as one ever since.

And Tiga figured out her mum is someone called Gretal Green, an inventor at NAPA (the

1

National Above the Pipes Association). Tiga's surname wasn't Whicabim at all; her evil guardian, Miss Heks – who kept her in a shed and made her drink mouldy old cheese water – had just made it up as a joke. All she had to go on was the fact she's actually from Silver City, Sinkville's second largest city, which has been deserted ever since the Big Exit. That's where she's planning to go next. That's where she thinks her mum must be.

Anyway, as they were all celebrating beating evil Felicity Bat, something weird happened. A wrinkly old hand emerged from the pipes and dropped an apple down to the dancing crowds, but everyone was having far too much fun to spot it.

It's the morning now, though, and Peggy has just spotted it …

1

That Apple

Tiga's big black patent rucksack swayed and sagged on her determined little back as she strolled briskly up Ritzy Avenue.

'Hi, Mavis!' she shouted.

Mavis waved as she unsuccessfully tried to stack one cat on top of another. Mavis had recently expanded her jam stall to include jam *and* cats. A fact Nottie, the only other jam *and* cats stall owner, was, frankly, livid about.

Some witches were sweeping the streets, clearing up the debris from the party the night before.

Onwards Tiga went, knocking on the window of Cakes, Pies and That's About It Really and waving up to Mrs Brew's studio window at the very top of the Brew's fashion boutique. Tiga knew Mrs Brew was tucked up

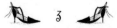

3

in bed with a very bad cold (and a gigantic toad on her face in a bid to cure it) and wasn't there. But she always liked to wave anyway.

'Tiga!' one of the Brew's witches shouted out of the window. 'Come on in for a natter!'

'I can't!' Tiga called over. She spun around and wiggled her backpack. 'I'm going on an adventure.'

The Brew's witch winked and began arranging some mannequins in the window.

Tiga began to pick up the pace. She couldn't be late. Peggy said she had to be there promptly …

'PEGS!' Tiga shouted as she reached Linden House. 'What the frognails are you doing?'

Peggy wiped her brow, straightened her glasses and grabbed the magnifying glass she had bewitched to hover over a strange little object on the street.

A couple of other witches had stopped to stare at it too. One of them was shouting, 'IT'S EVIL MAGIC! EVIL!'

'I'm confused,' Peggy finally said, as Tiga bent down and picked the thing up.

4

It was an apple.

She sniffed it.

It was definitely an apple.

'What?' Tiga said, tossing it back to Peggy (who dropped it and scuttled after it as it rolled slowly down the road). 'It's just an apple.'

'Is it?' Peggy asked.

'Definitely,' said Tiga.

More witches began to gather around and ooh and aah at it.

'Is this a joke?' Tiga asked. 'IT'S JUST AN APPLE!'

One witch tried to reach out and touch it. Peggy snatched it away.

'Look closely, Tiga,' Peggy said. 'Or just look, not even closely. What is strange about this apple?'

Tiga barely looked at it. 'That it's making you all NUTS?'

Peggy shook her head. 'Think about it.'

Tiga plucked the apple from her grasp and looked at it again. 'I just see a green apple.'

She gasped.

Peggy nodded knowingly.

'GREEN?!' Tiga cried. 'It's green! But all the colour went from Sinkville during the Big Exit.'

Peggy nodded as the apple, weirdly, began to glow. 'But now, for some strange reason, it seems to be coming back …'

Above the Pipes TV

In a crumbly old sitting room in the world above the pipes, sitting next to a moth-eaten armchair was an ancient TV set. It crackled and groaned as it struggled to stay switched on. The image on the screen blurred every so often and was struck through with irritating digital lines that broke up the image and made it jiggle.

Past the TV and outside beyond the window stood a crumbling shed that complemented the crumbling interior of the sitting room perfectly.

'Ooh,' said a woman outside. 'It's all very crumbly and matching, isn't it?'

Around her buzzed a camera crew – two cameramen and one sound guy. She cleared her throat and held a

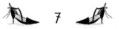

microphone up to her mouth. She was the same reporter who could be seen on the TV inside.

'We're here at the home of Miss Heks, a woman not many people in the community were friendly with. Only the cheese shop owner seemed to know anything about her. And the only thing he knew about her was that she was very fond of cheese.'

The camera shifted to the shed.

'This shed was where she kept her cheese. The cheese has in fact disappeared now, no one knows to where, but it is suspected it has gone wherever she and all the other women on this street have vanished to. And the twenty or so streets beyond it. Police forces are out and on the lookout for a couple of hundred or more old women, who dominated this area of the neighbourhood.'

The picture on the TV shifted to various photographs of old women with crooked noses and warty faces. And then back to the reporter outside Miss Heks's shed.

'Speculation is rife as to where they may be. However, we ask the community to remain calm. They

can't have got very far … because their legs are very, very old.

'More on this story as it develops. Now back to Arthur in the studio.'

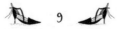

The Return of Miss Heks

'Cooey!' came a voice.

'I wonder why the colour is back?' Tiga said to Peggy, as Fluffanora strolled up to them.

'Ready for our Silver City adventure?' she said with a smile. 'Wait, GREEN! Why is the apple green?'

'Cooey!'

Peggy shrugged. 'I have no idea. Nothing else seems to be in colour, just this apple ... and it's glowing ... like magic.'

'Most things are magic in this place ...' Tiga mumbled. 'COOEY.'

Peggy put it in her pocket. 'I'm going to hide it in Linden House until I can figure out what it is and why it's glowing.'

10

'COOEY! HOW MANY TIMES DO I NEED TO SAY COOEY?!'

Tiga spun around and then fell over. Her legs had buckled when she saw it.

Standing there like she had been there all along was someone completely terrible. A vibrant dash of fluorescent orange in a garishly glittery dress, topped with a clashing gold hat.

It was Miss Heks, her old evil guardian.

'More colour!' Peggy gasped.

'Oh,' Miss Heks said, changing her voice to the littlest little whimper in an attempt to sound sweet. It sounded like something evil squashed in a small hole.

'Oh, my Tiga. You have been lost for so long!'

'*Lost?*' said Fluffanora, as she bit into a Cakes, Pies and That's About It Really pie. 'You let us adopt her. I was there.'

'Ah, this must be why the colour's coming back,' Peggy said, her eyes darting from colourful Miss Heks to the green apple tucked in her pocket and back again.

'Go away!' Tiga blurted out.

11

Miss Heks's face scrunched up, like it always did before she screamed and shouted. But she just swallowed, like she was swallowing a lump of something spiky.

'Oh well,' she said in a strained voice. 'I suppose you did adopt her, but I've changed my mind. I miss her, you see.'

Tiga's eyes widened and she took a step backwards. Fluffanora and Peggy linked arms with her.

A glittery ball BURST on to the scene.

'ALL THE GANG BACK TOGETHER!' Fran oozed. 'Oh dear, that is BRIGHT,' she said, pointing at Miss Heks. She waved her hand and some ridiculously fluffy sunglasses appeared on Tiga, Peggy and Fluffanora's faces. Fluffanora, without a moment's thought, whipped them off and threw them over her head. Tiga and Peggy kept theirs on for a couple more seconds, so as not to offend Fran ...

'Listen, I don't want to be a pain. I'd just like to spend some time with Tiga,' Miss Heks went on.

'This isn't right,' Tiga whispered to Peggy. 'There's a reason she's back, I know it.'

Peggy nodded. 'What do we do?'

'I can't hear either of you,' Fluffanora whispered.

They huddled together.

'What if she follows us around everywhere?' Tiga asked. 'What if she tries to take me back up there?'

'And what about the adventure to Silver City?' Fluffanora added. 'Miss Heks can't know we're trying to find your mum. She never mentioned her to you in all the years you lived with her. She said she found you in the sink in the shed. She's a liar …'

They all turned slowly to look at her as some trumpets sounded.

'What is this silly show?' Fran said, pointing at the band that had materialised next to Miss Heks. They were obviously something she had bewitched because they looked like ghost witches. Tiga could see right through them. The music got louder and louder and Miss Heks began dancing down the street towards Tiga.

She was all elbows and ankles.

'Oh my sweetest Tiga, I have missed you ever so,' she sang in a creepy old voice.

She flicked her finger and the music paused.

13

'Many timeeeees I've cried a tear, at the thought of letting you goooooooooooo.'

She flicked her finger and the music blared once more! Witches started dancing along beside her.

'OI! STOP MAKING US DANCE!' they cried.

'TIGA, YOU ARE THE GREATEST, I LOVE YOUR LITTLE TOES!'

'You have quite big toes, actually …' Fluffanora said.

'YOUR SQUISHY FACE, YOUR LOVELY HAIR, YOUR BUTTON LITTLE NOOOOOSE!'

'I'm scared,' Peggy said.

'TIGA, I HAVE MISSED YOU MOOORE, MORE THAN A GENTLE BREEZE!

MORE THAN A SPELL!

A FROG!

OR A CAT!

EVEN MOREEEEE …

THAN CHEEEEEESE.'

'Well, that's a lie,' Tiga said.

'IF YOU WILL NOT COME BACK WITH ME, BACK TO OUR LOVELY HOME.'

'I wouldn't call it lovely. Mouldy, perhaps. Or grim. Not lovely,' Fran said.

The reluctant dancing witches followed behind Miss Heks, mouthing 'Sorry', and 'She's making my legs move.'

The band began to slow.

'THEN MAYBE I CAN STAY DOWN HERE SO I WON'T FEEL SO ...'

She tried her best to sound sad:

'ALONE.'

The band disappeared with a pop and Fran accidentally clapped.

'Although she is terrifying, *that* was an impressive show. Good choreography! Bravo!'

Tiga glared at Fran and she stopped yelling compliments.

Slowly, Tiga stepped closer to Miss Heks, eyeing her suspiciously.

'You can't stay here,' Tiga said firmly. 'For a start, there's nowhere for you to live.'

Miss Heks looked up and down the avenue and

tapped her foot. 'In that case, I think I'll just bring my old house back.'

She flicked her finger, and up above the pipes, the TV crew outside her house gasped as the entire thing vanished. The TV reporter leaned against the shed to steady herself.

'GOLLY! What is going *on*?'

And then the shed disappeared too.

'I'll just stick it … here,' Miss Heks said, as her tatty old house wiggled its way down from the pipe and squeezed in beside the Brews' house on pristine Ritzy Avenue.

'That's, well, OK …' Peggy mumbled.

Miss Heks trotted towards her house. 'Anyone for cheese water?'

'OH NOT THIS NONSENSE AGAIN!' Fran cried as a very familiar crumbly old shed landed with a bang in front of Tiga.

WARWOP!

The witches of *WARWOP!* magazine (Witches Around Ritzy Who Often Panic) have some PANIC-INDUCING news for you.

As you may have heard, colour is back in Ritzy City – Peggy found a green apple. THIS IS SERIOUS and can only mean one thing ... DON'T PANIC, *but* rumours are rife that Celia Crayfish, the most evil witch ever to rule Sinkville, is planning a return to Ritzy City! Her fellow Big Exit witch Miss Heks has already reappeared, with cheese, and we think Celia Crayfish is going to arrive next.

There have been a number of sightings of her – most of them have been by panicking witches who keep seeing the old statue of Celia Crayfish near the market and mistaking it for her. We hung a sign on the statue that said THIS IS A STATUE to avoid confusion, but then we just got reports saying Celia Crayfish is back and has disguised herself with a sign that says THIS IS A STATUE. So ... that didn't work.

If Celia Crayfish is on her way back, then WE

MUST FIND OUT WHERE SHE IS WHEN SHE GETS HERE SO WE CAN MAKE SURE WE CAN HIDE FROM HER!

MOST IMPORTANTLY PLEASE REMEMBER TO PANIC RESPONSIBLY!!!

For all panic-related enquiries, please contact Mavis, Jam (And Sometimes Cats) Stall Number 9.

Keep Your Evil
Guardians Closer ...

'On second thoughts,' Tiga said, as she looked up from the *WARWOP!* article that had just been handed to her by a panicking witch, 'maybe we should let Miss Heks hang out with us. She's obviously up to something. If it's linked to the Big Exit witches and Celia Crayfish, we need to find out what it is – and fast.'

'Keep your friends close and your evil guardians closer,' Fluffanora said with a satisfied grin.

'Very clever,' Peggy said. 'Are you *sure*, Tiga? This will make going to Silver City to look for your mum much trickier.'

Tiga watched as Miss Heks skipped towards them. 'I'm not sure I have much of a choice ...'

'She's trying to skip so she looks friendly, isn't she?'

Fluffanora said, as Miss Heks's knobbly legs smacked against each other, sending her careering across the street.

Tiga sighed as the old bat tripped, forward rolled and landed in a spindly heap in front of her.

'Ta da!' Miss Heks said as she got to her feet.

Fran clapped loudly as Tiga looked up into the sky. Above her, the pipes swirled with bright colours. She shivered. It felt like something really bad was readying to fall down from up there …

5

Inside the Gull & Chip Tavern

'Oooh, Fel-Fel, something is going on out there!' Aggie Hoof squealed, jumping up and down by the only window in the Gull & Chip Tavern. She was waving her new magazine. Ever since Darcy Dream, the editor of *Toad*, had bewitched the magazine so it would shoot slime at Aggie Hoof and steal her shoes if she ever read it, she had had to resort to reading the much less cool fashion magazine, *Frock*, written by seven-hundred-year-old Anastasia Lumpley, who was so old she'd forgotten how to string sentences together, causing much confusion among her readers.

'Wear skirts FROGBATS when skipping TOES. Nice glitter!' Aggie Hoof read aloud, sounding completely lost. 'Midnight jackets, SOUP!'

Felicity Bat sat in the shadows trying to ignore her. She was sipping the only drink available in the place – Crubbly. Rumour was if you were properly evil, it would taste like tears. If you weren't evil at all, it just tasted like lemonade.

'Fel-Fel, do you think it's true what those WARWOP witches say about your gran coming back? Maybe she's coming back because we've been rubbish at being evil!'

Felicity Bat threw her glass across the room. It smashed against a large portrait of Celia Crayfish herself.

'We are *excellently* evil,' Felicity Bat said. 'I'm the best at being the worst. Everyone is terrified of me.'

Aggie Hoof shook her head and tossed her *Frock* magazine over her shoulder. 'Not since you unsuccessfully tried to take over Linden House. And yesterday, when you levitated into that lamp post … and then there was that time you –'

'QUUUUUIIIIIEEEEEETTTTTT!' Felicity Bat screeched.

Nasty Nancy, the owner of the Gull & Chip Tavern, stared at them from the bar with a disapproving gaze.

'I think we need to rethink our image,' Aggie Hoof said.

'WILL YOU BE QUIET, I'M THINKING!' Felicity Bat snapped. She spun around and her long plait got caught in her mouth. She spat it out and stood very still.

'What, Fel-Fel?'

Felicity Bat grinned, flicked her finger and a pair of scissors appeared.

She began chopping.

'Um, Fel-Fel?'

Within seconds Felicity Bat's hair was short and spiky.

Aggie Hoof held up the limp long plait that had been attached to Felicity Bat's head. And then she threw it across the room because it freaked her out.

'We need to do something evil. We need to fix this. I mean, look at us all,' Felicity Bat said as she pointed around the room at all the hunched and mean and terrifying witches that littered the place. 'We're the best-worst Sinkville has to offer and we're huddled away in this tiny tavern doing *nothing*.'

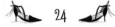

'Well, Fel-Fel, not nothing – you did just cut your hair …'

Felicity Bat ignored her. 'We need to get out there and make this place evil agai–'

Before she could finish, there was a loud bang and smoke filled the room.

'I TOLD YOU NOT TO DO ANY SPELLS USING OLD FINGERS!' they heard Nasty Nancy yell. 'THEY ALWAYS SMOKE THE PLACE OUT!'

But it wasn't anyone using old fingers for spells. As the smoke cleared, Felicity Bat could make out a message floating in the air.

BE HERE, JUST BEFORE DAWN.
OH, EVIL WILL BE BACK ALL RIGHT.

'Who's doing that writing, Fel-Fel?'

Nasty Nancy clutched her heart and grinned.

'Fel-Fel, answer me, who is doing that writing?'

Felicity Bat stared at it in disbelief. She recognised the writing. She knew exactly who had sent the message.

Aggie Hoof stroked her chin. 'And who is Dawn?'

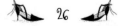

Norma Milton

Tiga sat across from Miss Heks as she picked at a pie in Cakes, Pies and That's About It Really, the baker's.

Every witch in the place was staring at the old bat in her luminous orange dress, their mouths open.

'Well, this is nice!' Miss Heks said, picking some pie out of her teeth and flicking it across the room.

Tiga couldn't resist. 'Why are you *really* here?'

'To see you, of course!'

Tiga looked to the window, where Fluffanora and Peggy were standing outside, holding *Toad* magazines up to their faces. They had cut eyeholes in them so it looked like they were reading but really they were spying. Fluffanora's one was convincing, but Peggy had

27

made the eyeholes too big, so you could see most of her face …

'But you hate me,' Tiga went on. 'You left me in the shed with only a slug to play with.'

'You don't still have that slug, do you?' Miss Heks asked casually. Almost too casually.

Tiga thought for a moment. 'No,' she lied. 'It died.'

Miss Heks smiled. 'Oh well, they do that sometimes.'

A young witch waitress who looked about Tiga's age strolled over. 'Can I get you anything else?'

Tiga shook her head. 'No, thanks.'

'I'm Norma Milton, by the way,' the witch waitress said. Tiga noticed the edge of her dress was purple. A couple of the cake stands in Cakes, Pies and That's About It Really had started to get their colour back too and were turning pink.

'Hello, Norma Milton,' Miss Heks replied.

Norma Milton pulled up a chair and sat down with them. A witch at the next table threw her hands in the air and shouted, 'Oi! We're ready to order!' But Norma Milton didn't seem to care.

'It's great to meet you, Tiga. I watched *Witch Wars* and you were excellent.'

'Wasn't she?!' Miss Heks said with a forced smile.

Tiga shifted awkwardly in her chair. 'Are you new to Ritzy City?' she asked Norma. 'I haven't seen you in here before.'

Norma Milton nodded enthusiastically. 'I'm from the Towers. Actually, you ran past my tower when you were

29

in *Witch Wars*. It was very exciting! Oh, and is that Peggy out there? And Fluffanora!' She stood up and gestured for them to come in.

Peggy dropped her magazine and looked shocked, as Fluffanora rolled up hers and hit Peggy with it. 'I *told you* you made the eyeholes too big!' Tiga heard her say as they stumbled through the door.

'Wow, all three of you in one place,' Norma Milton said as she introduced herself to Fluffanora and Peggy. Tiga watched her intently as she smiled sweetly and told Peggy what a wonderful ruling witch she was, and how much she loved Fluffanora's hat.

Peggy grinned. 'You must come over sometime soon and I can show you around Linden House!'

'Oh, I'd love that!' Norma Milton said with a squeal.

Miss Heks snorted. She'd fallen asleep.

'Niceness bores her,' Tiga whispered as she slowly tried to get up.

The chair squeaked and Miss Heks jolted awake. 'CRIME!' she sleepily shouted.

'Would you like some tea?' Norma Milton asked.

'You should try one of the tarts,' Miss Heks said, blowing her nose on Norma Milton's apron.

'So sorry,' Tiga mouthed.

Norma Milton smiled awkwardly.

'Girls!' Mrs Brew cried as she shot through the door, followed by Fran. She was clutching a large black rag covered in gloop, her hair was uncharacteristically ALL OVER THE PLACE and she was in a little nightdress. 'I have been looking everywhere for you. There's a lopsided old house next to ours. Do you have any idea why it's –'

She stopped. Her face crumpled. 'Miss *Heks*?'

'Mum, what are you doing?!' Fluffanora snapped. 'Get back home to bed right now. You're not well.'

'You're back?' Mrs Brew said, sneezing all over Miss Heks.

Fran was busily hovering behind her, sneakily trying to rearrange her hair.

'I just wanted to see Tiga,' Miss Heks said. 'She has made it very clear that she doesn't want to come and live with me, so I decided to move back. I put my house next to yours – we're neighbours!'

Mrs Brew raised an eyebrow. 'You just decided to come back?'

'That must be why the apple was green,' Peggy said. 'Miss Heks, being a Big Exit witch and everything, has brought some of the colour back with her. Look at the cake stands, and Norma's dress.'

Fran sneezed.

'Oh, Fran, you must be ill too,' Mrs Brew said.

Fran thought for a moment. 'I'm not going to *die*, am I? Because I'm very important. There will be no one to present *Cooking for Tiny People*!'

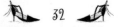 32

She flew about the room in a fluster, screeching, 'I MUST GO OOOOOOON!' then smacked into a wall and slid to the ground.

'Well, I'd better be off too. I don't want to get sick!' Norma Milton chirped.

She hugged Peggy goodbye and headed out of the door.

'She's great!' Peggy said.

'Um … I thought she was the waitress … ?' Fluffanora said to no one in particular, but none of them were listening.

'Come on, girls,' Mrs Brew said, ushering them away from Miss Heks. 'Time to go home.'

Tiga felt Mrs Brew's arm wrapped tightly around her. She looked back before she stepped out of the door. Miss Heks was grinning and waving, her spindly fingers wiggling slowly like old worms.

Tiga shivered.

'Something is not right here,' Mrs Brew whispered in Tiga's ear.

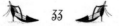

7

Brooms

Later that evening, Mrs Brew sat down with them and sneezed her way through all the reasons why Miss Heks might be back. She was more worried than anyone. They had been discussing it for so long, it was now the middle of the night.

'She could *SNEEZE* genuinely miss you … Or *SNEEZE* have gone a bit mad – perhaps all the *SNEEZE* cheese water has turned her good? I bet she's up to something. She *SNEEZE* must be.'

'I don't want her to get in the way of our trip to Silver City. We *have* to keep looking for my mum,' Tiga said, stroking the slug. 'You know, Miss Heks was asking me about my slug,' she added.

'She's going to notice if we trot off down the road to

Silver City; her crumbly old house is just next door,'
Fluffanora said, pulling back the curtain to reveal Miss
Heks's house. A crooked nose was poking out of the
window.

'See,' Fluffanora said. 'She's watching.'

The slug buried its beehive of hair under Tiga's thumb.

'She's going to hold everything up,' Tiga moaned.
'I want to go to Silver City *now*.'

Peggy patted her on the back.

'I have an idea *SNEEZE!*' Mrs Brew said, leaping to
her feet and waving her hands in the air.

'I'm worried about her sanity ...' Fluffanora mumbled.

Mrs Brew continued to wave her arms as Tiga
looked on.

'Bristles and bush and three seats smoosh,' Mrs Brew
mumbled. 'Here in three, two, one ... WHOOSH.'

Peggy dived under the bed!

Fluffanora ducked.

And Tiga ... well, she was knocked to the ground by
the bristly, bushy broom that came careering into the
room.

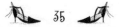

35

She leapt back up, raised an arm in the air and shouted, 'I'M FINE!'

Mrs Brew grabbed the broom and held it steady. 'You can take it to the attic window and sail out high above the houses. That old bat Miss Heks will never see you. I'll distract her tomorrow morning – say you're all in bed with the flu. That'll buy you some time.'

'Will we all fit?' Fluffanora asked as she eyed the broom wiggling in front of her.

'It's a three-seater broom, Fluffanora,' Mrs Brew said. 'There's plenty of room.'

Tiga took hold of the broom and with her other hand she slipped the slug into her pocket.

Mrs Pumpkin, the cat, growled from under the bed.

'Bye, Pumpkin Head!' Fluffanora said.

'You know she hates being called that,' Mrs Brew said, as Mrs Pumpkin produced a single claw and waved it in Fluffanora's direction.

Peggy grabbed hold of the broom too. And then Fluffanora.

'Follow the floating lanterns west,' Mrs Brew said.

'All the way, you hear, past the perfect line of trees until you see the silver stilts of Silver City sticking through the clouds. You should be there before morning.'

Tiga lifted the broom meaningfully in the air, '*This* is the start of our epic jour–'

SMACK!

She hit Peggy in the face with the handle.

'Oh, frogcrutches, so sorry, Peggy!'

Peggy held her nose. 'Nope, it's fine, just my nose …
Who needs a nose! I can, I don't know, breathe through
my mouth …'

8

Linden House Light

It was a cool, clear night and Tiga could hear the distant sound of clinking glasses from Clutterbucks and witches chattering in the near darkness on their way home. It was late and most of Ritzy City was tucked up in bed. Lights flickered behind bedroom curtains and one by one went out. Miss Heks's house was completely dark now.

'Wait for it,' Fluffanora said as the lanterns that lined the streets were extinguished at once.

'Go!' she whispered as the three of them shot out of the attic window of 99 Ritzy Avenue and soared high above the rooftops.

'Hey!' Peggy shouted. 'Look over there at Linden House – the sitting-room light is on!'

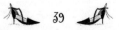

'Maybe you left it on,' Fluffanora shouted back to Peggy.

'Or maybe it's your glowing apple?' Tiga said.

Peggy stared down at the huge building, her nose wrinkled – partly because she was thinking and partly because she still had some broom bristles stuck in it.

And then the most peculiar thing happened.

'Hey! The light went out!' Peggy cried. 'Who switched it on? And *who* just switched it off?'

Tiga and Fluffanora glanced back at Linden House.

Tiga tried to focus her eyes as they whizzed through the air. She twisted around on the broom for a better look. She was sure she could see a figure climbing out of the back window! She squinted and turned again as the figure scuttled through the garden.

'There's someone there!' Tiga shouted.

'Where?' Fluffanora demanded.

Tiga pointed but the others couldn't see anything.

'Oh, it's probably nothing,' Peggy said. 'Or it's Pat the chef.'

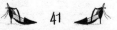

Tiga nodded even though she wasn't convinced. She leaned back further on the broom and watched as Linden House and all of Ritzy City faded into the distance.

The Watch

Felicity Bat paced back and forth in the Gull & Chip Tavern.

Every pair of eyes in the place followed her.

Back and forth.

Back and forth.

The doors had been bolted by Nasty Nancy.

In the middle stood a terrifying figure clad in a bright purple dress.

'CELIA CRAYFISH,' Nasty Nancy oozed as Felicity Bat tried to hug her gran.

'I really thought you were gone above the pipes for ever,' Felicity Bat rambled.

Celia Crayfish flicked a finger and sent her flying. 'No hugging, Felicity,' she said coldly. 'I've been

43

hearing all about you. What a ghastly disappointment you are.'

Only those in her inner circle had been allowed inside. That included Miss Heks, who had scuttled along to say hi to her friend. She'd brought stinking cheese, so everyone hated her. Then there was Nasty Nancy, who was whipping up drinks for everyone; Felicity, who Celia Crayfish seemed determined to insult every couple of seconds; and Aggie Hoof, who, frankly, was close to being killed by the recently returned witch.

'Ooooh, I like your evil shoes, Celia Crayfish,' Aggie Hoof said.

'What did you say?' Celia Crayfish snapped, her face scrunched up and shaking in fury. She looked like a paper bag that had just eaten a squirrel.

Felicity Bat nudged Aggie Hoof and urgently shook her head.

'Um …' Aggie Hoof said, looking from Felicity Bat to Celia Crayfish. '… Nothing. I said nothing.'

Celia Crayfish growled and carried on pacing the room. It was beginning to grow light outside.

'Witches, this is a crucial moment in the history of Sinkville,' she said, her voice crackling like an old radio. 'This is the moment when we take over Sinkville once and for all.'

'But there's only about two of us!' Aggie Hoof said.

'There's *five*,' Celia Crayfish said with a sigh. 'Really, Felicity, you couldn't even get a decent sidekick.'

Felicity Bat stared at her feet and then up at Miss Heks, who – arguably – was a *worse* sidekick.

'I have spent *years* above the pipes,' Celia Crayfish went on, 'studying how they do things. Some of the things they do are *really* bad. Children up there are terrified of us! Terrified! They see us coming and they cross the street. They don't have magic, you see! They are powerless. Not like the kids down here, with all their power, ruling the place! Children,' she spat. 'RULING THE PLACE!'

'But you ruled the place when you were a child,' Felicity Bat pointed out.

Celia Crayfish sighed. 'And I deserved to rule because I was special, but then I had to stop because I got older

45

and this stupid little world only lets young people rule! I left this place – it's no good for old people. But up there, in the world above the pipes, being old is wonderful! People think you know everything, and children have to do what you say! It's HEAVEN.'

Aggie Hoof looked confused. 'You mean children don't get to make the laws?'

Celia Crayfish cackled so loudly the roof of the tavern shook. 'No! They think it's –' she paused and grinned a fang-ridden grin – 'ridiculous! They think it's ridiculous to trust kids with things like laws. Oh, it's just a magical world up there!'

She took a seat. 'But now I'm back. And it's time we made Sinkville like the world up there. I'm going to make this place evil again, and I'm going to put young witches in their rightful place! I AM GOING TO RULE THIS LAND WITH MY WRINKLY HANDS! I WILL TERRIFY CHILDREN! I WILL WIN.'

'But you're *not a child*,' Aggie Hoof said.

Celia Crayfish cackled. 'EXACTLY.'

'You don't think children are good enough?' Felicity Bat asked.

'NEVER!' Celia Crayfish roared. 'In a couple of days this place will be under my control once again!'

'How are you going to do it, Granny? How will you take over?' Felicity Bat asked.

'IT'S CELIA CRAYFISH TO YOU,' she snapped. 'Until you can prove your worth.'

She rolled back her sleeve to reveal a large watch.

It was huge and beautiful, with sculpted edges that looked like twisted thorny branches. Felicity Bat stared at it in amazement. She had studied everything about her gran, and her watch was the best bit!

Celia Crayfish cackled. 'Before we sent Tiga down for Witch Wars, we bewitched her, so with this watch we could see whatever she saw. It was like having a little roving camera moving around the place. I saw your pathetic battle scene at the end of Witch Wars, Felicity. I saw it.'

'Why didn't you just sneak back and see what was going on?' Aggie Hoof asked.

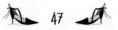

'Because,' Celia Crayfish said in a mocking voice, 'we'd stolen all the colour, hadn't we? So if we sneaked back, all the colour would come back too.'

Aggie Hoof scratched her head. 'But you're back now and all the colour is coming back …'

Miss Heks took a step forward and interrupted. 'Yes, but everyone thinks it's because of me. Little old me returning to see Tiga because I –' she swallowed and looked disgusted – '*miss* her. No one knows Celia is back too.'

'The WARWOP witches think you're back – they are *on* to you,' Aggie Hoof pointed out.

A bead of sweat dribbled down Felicity Bat's spindly nose. She widened her eyes at Aggie Hoof to warn her to be quiet.

Celia Crayfish just shrugged. 'It's probably the first time the WARWOP witches have panicked correctly. But the thing is, most witches think they're insane, and so the more they rant about me being back, the less people are likely to believe it! Oh, they'll get such a fright when they see all the other Big Exit witches have returned too.'

49

Felicity Bat and Aggie Hoof both gasped and looked around.

'They aren't *here*,' Celia Crayfish said. 'Well, not yet. They are sneaking back – one by one. Miss Heks is hiding as many of them as she can fit in her house after they drop down from the pipes.'

Miss Heks gave a satisfied grunt.

'No one will go near her house – they can't stand the stink of the cheese!' Celia Crayfish finished with a cackle.

'So, wait, you sent Tiga to win Witch Wars so Miss Heks could come and pretend to visit her and you could sneak every bad witch back before anyone could stop you?' Felicity Bat rambled.

'Yes, everyone thinking it's just Miss Heks buys us some time. We needed to find a way to get everyone through the pipes before anyone figures out what we're up to and tries to block them shut.'

'But Tiga didn't win Witch Wars,' Felicity Bat said slowly.

'That's right,' Celia Crayfish said, getting to her feet

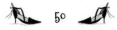

and pacing the room again, 'but luckily that Piggy and the Brew girl wanted her to stay with them for ever and came to get her.'

'That was a stroke of luck!' Miss Heks said with a snort.

'We knew she was the best contestant in Witch Wars, even without spells; we had no idea she would give in and let Piggy win,' Celia Crayfish said.

Felicity Bat's face crumpled. 'You didn't think I would win?'

'*Please*, Felicity,' Celia Crayfish snapped. 'Of course not.' She tapped the watch. 'Something is wrong with this.'

The face of the watch was misty and glowed dimly.

'It's a live feed of Tiga's view,' Celia Crayfish said, as Felicity Bat and Aggie Hoof peered intently at it. 'Whatever she sees, we see.'

The image was hazy; they could barely make it out at all. It looked a lot like Peggy clutching on to a broom. The view swivelled to reveal Fluffanora, also clutching on to a broom, her hair everywhere.

'They're on a broom,' Celia Crayfish said.

'What?' Miss Heks asked. 'But they should be in bed, shouldn't they?'

The view shifted to Tiga's hand reaching inside her pocket and patting the slug.

'You said the slug was dead, Eggweena!' Celia Crayfish screamed, grabbing Miss Heks by her collar.

'Eggweena?' Felicity Bat said with a smirk.

'That's … that's what the brat told me!' Miss Heks stammered.

'Where could they be going?' Celia Crayfish demanded.

Miss Heks stared at her blankly. 'I … I just don't … know, Your Gloriousness …'

'They're probably sneaking off to Silver City,' Felicity Bat said, rolling her eyes.

'Silver City?!' Celia Crayfish screeched, shaking the watch. 'SHE MUST NOT GO TO SILVER CITY! Why are they going there?'

'I think they might be trying to find Tiga's mum,' Felicity Bat explained. 'They found out she's Gretal

Green.' She tried to touch the watch but Celia Crayfish slapped her hand away.

'SHE MUST NOT DO THAT! This is more serious than I thought, Eggweena. She must not figure out what happened to the other witches, especially that Gretal Green at NAPA. If they find her, she could stop us with her clever magic!'

The image began to flicker. Celia Crayfish screamed.

'Why is the image disappearing?' Aggie Hoof asked. 'Look at it! It's almost gone!'

The watch face exploded. Celia Crayfish screamed and frantically shook her wrist.

'Oooh, look at that mess,' Aggie Hoof said, pointing at the little watch bits littering the floor.

'They're nearing Silver City – that area is heavily protected from outside spy magic! Aaargh, those meddling witches at NAPA made sure of it! This watch took years to perfect. YEARS.' Celia Crayfish gave Miss Heks a knowing look. 'Someone needs to stop them snooping in Silver City – they could ruin everything.'

'I'll do it!' Felicity Bat cried. 'I can do it!'

Celia Crayfish thought about that for a moment. She walked up to her granddaughter and lowered her voice. 'In Gretal Green's office in NAPA, you will find an important piece of paper containing slug instructions.'

'Slug instructions,' Felicity Bat repeated slowly.

'S-l-u-g i-n-s-t-r-u-c-t-i-o-n-s. Bring it to me. Do not let Tiga see it. It is of the utmost importance that she does not see it. Get it and then GET THEM OUT OF THERE.'

Felicity Bat nodded.

'This is your one and only chance to prove yourself, Felicity,' Celia Crayfish said quietly. 'Don't mess it up.'

Felicity Bat nodded again as, just behind her, where no one was looking, a little beehive of perfectly groomed fairy hair slowly ducked down below the window.

'Fabulous Fran has now seen that Celia Crayfish is definitely back,' Fran whispered to herself, pretending she was narrating a film about her own life. 'What will Fabulous Fran do next? Dun! Dun! Duuun!'

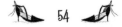

To Silver City

The cool air gently whooshed past Tiga's face, sending her hair flying all over the place.

She dug her nails into the hard wood of the old broom. Peggy was in front of her leading the way, and Fluffanora was elegantly perched on the end, peering down as dawn was breaking over Sinkville.

Ahead of them was a swirling darkness, with only the occasional lantern floating in the air to light their way.

As they pressed on, they passed signs every so often. They were crumbly and old-fashioned-looking.

'No one uses these routes any more,' Peggy called back. 'No need to now that all the other cities are deserted.'

It was silent up there, just the occasional creak of an old sign, pointing the way to Silver City, Driptown and beyond.

Tiga looked up into the pipes that hung above them. Inside swirled bright colours – green, purple, orange, yellow, red – like they were all ready to fall down and coat the place in colour.

'Do you think the colour is like that because Miss Heks is back?' Tiga said.

Peggy shrugged. 'I suppose so. She is a Big Exit witch. It would make sense that the colour is seeping back.'

'But why so much of it?' Fluffanora asked. 'You're telling me one Big Exit witch is causing all the colour to come back? I'm with the WARWOP witches. I think it's Celia Crayfish.'

'But the WARWOP witches are notorious panickers,' Peggy said. 'Remember that time they thought the cats were conspiring to eat us all?'

'Oh, I liked that article a lot,' Fluffanora said. 'What was it called again?'

'CATS CAN HOLD FORKS; DON'T BELIEVE THEIR LIES,' Peggy said, rolling her eyes.

'That's the one,' Fluffanora said.

Tiga just stared at them.

They passed a floating platform that had little lights dotted around the edge. A sign, as crumbly as the others, read TAKE A BROOM BREAK. RECHARGE YOUR FEATHER DUSTERS HERE.

Peggy leaned to her right and the broom guided them towards the platform. As they got closer, Tiga could see a small building perched on it.

'It looks a little like a garage where people above the pipes fill up their cars with petrol,' Tiga said.

Fluffanora cackled. 'Sometimes you don't make any sense at all.'

Peggy giggled.

The broom swooped down and landed on the platform, which wobbled a bit. They jumped off and it sailed away all by itself and slotted into a rack in the corner. It glowed.

'You need to give them a rest or they fall out of the sky,' Peggy explained as Tiga shot the broom a terrified glance.

Fluffanora opened the door to the little building, which seemed to be made of a weird black plastic.

Inside it was eerily empty. A staircase snaked around the edge, leading to various balconies that housed cafés and places to rest. On the ground floor, there was nothing but a pile of chairs stacked in the corner, alongside some old copies of the *Ritzy City Post*. Tiga picked one up and it almost disintegrated in her hand.

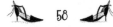

WITCHES LEAVE SINKVILLE. WHY? (SERIOUSLY, READERS, WHY? WE DON'T KNOW)

Today witches across the land began to vanish, taking everything with them to the world above the pipes.

'I just don't know why the frogs they would do that!' said Mrs Clutterbuck, whose two sisters, the other Mrs Clutterbucks, were among those who left. They had only recently moved to Driptown to open a new Clutterbucks café there.

Many have taken their houses, shops and sheds with them, but others, such as the majority of those in Silver City, left everything behind. There have been reports of missing houses in Ritzy City, and many in the Docks have vanished. No one remains in Silver City or Driptown and beyond – just their hats.

Fluffanora unstacked the chairs and started putting them back where they would've been. 'Places like this used to be really buzzy, I bet. Lots of witches milling around, chatting and talking about their travels. Now look at it. Boring and empty.'

'Who you calling boring?' a voice said.

The three of them jumped and looked up. There, on the very top balcony, was an extremely old witch. An old witch they recognised.

'It's the old cart witch!' Tiga cried.

The cart witch leapt off the balcony and landed with a thud next to them.

'Oh, my old knees,' she groaned.

'What are *you* doing here?' Peggy asked.

'This is where I store my hats. I used to always come here to collect 'em. It's the closest point to the pipes, you see. Lots of hats would fall on the roof and I'd pick 'em up and put 'em in my cart.'

She took a seat and flicked her finger. All the chairs Fluffanora had unstacked flew back into the corner.

'No need for them chairs. No one comes here any more … apart from you lot.'

'Who you knew would come here because you know everything …' Tiga said.

The old cart witch grinned.

'And you were right about the prophecy! Almost …' Peggy said. 'You mentioned something about an apple!'

> '*An elegant witch will rule this land,*
> *And that bossy one will lend a hand.*
> *Witch sisters, maybe, but not the same.*
> *One is dear.*
> *The other? A PAIN.*
> *And, much like the tales of times gone by,*
> *They will find a sweet apple and … My oh my, is that*
> *   the time? I'd better go.'*

Tiga recited it. She knew it off by heart. 'Is the apple important?' she asked eagerly.

'I'm not elegant, so does that mean someone takes over from me as the Top Witch?' Peggy asked nervously.

The old cart witch cackled. 'You will see, very soon. Things are not so black and white these days, are they?'

'You mean the colour that's seeping back,' Tiga said. 'Why is that happening? Is it because Miss Heks is back? Because of the apple?'

The old cart witch cackled. 'I aint tellin' you more than I already told you. And what I already told you is everything you need to know.'

'But you didn't even finish the apple bit, you just walked off!' Fluffanora protested.

'GENUINE WITCH HATS WOT GOT STUCK IN THE PIPES!' the cart witch started to shout.

'Oh, here she goes,' Fluffanora said, rolling her eyes.

'GENUINE WITCH HATS WOT GOT STUCK IN THE PIPES.'

And then she disappeared with a bang.

Mop

Felicity Bat levitated as her hapless sidekick tried to balance on the old mop Nasty Nancy had given her.

Miss Heks's shoulders bounced about as she sniggered. 'You're useless, Aggie Hoof.'

'Leave the mop, I'll carry you,' Felicity Bat said defensively. She didn't like anyone being mean to Aggie Hoof. That was *her* job.

'I'VE GOT THIS UNDER CONTROL!' Aggie Hoof shouted, doing a loop-the-loop and stopping nose to nose with Celia Crayfish.

'YOU ARE AN EMBARRASSMENT! BOTH OF YOU,' the evil witch bellowed, her warty nose wobbling dangerously close to Aggie Hoof's eye.

She turned
and marched
across the
room, tossing
a bright
green apple
from one hand
to the other.

'Is that the apple
Peggy had before?'
Aggie Hoof dared to ask.
'I saw her with it through
the window. Why did she have it?'

'Doesn't matter,' Celia Crayfish said casually. 'I
have it now.'

'How did you get it?' Felicity Bat asked as Aggie Hoof
got control of the mop and rose slowly into the air.

'Let's just say,' Celia Crayfish said with a grin, 'I have
a little helper ...'

Feet

Peggy snorted and snored. She was slumped over the front of the broom, snoozing. Tiga did the steering as Fluffanora napped against her back.

It was getting brighter and the signs for Silver City were becoming more frequent now. They soared lower, past one that read REMEMBER, YOU NEED A BOAT TO ENTER SILVER CITY.

In the distance, sticking through the clouds, were silver stilts as glittery as an excited Fran. The clouds parted and Tiga could see the swirl of silver liquid down below them. She tipped the broom forward slightly and they began their descent.

The bright silver buildings of the city came into view, huddled in the middle of the swirling silver river. Most

of them were round and of varying heights, supported by sparkling silver stilts. Walkways connected them all.

It looked so familiar to Tiga.

'SILVER CITY!' she shouted, waking the other two, who both nearly fell off the broom.

They passed another sign about Silver City and needing a boat.

'FROGBITS!' Peggy shouted. 'I *knew* I forgot something.'

'You forgot an entire boat?' Fluffanora said, an eyebrow raised.

'To be fair, you could've noticed that I had forgotten an entire boat,' Peggy pointed out.

Fluffanora shrugged.

'We could try a spell?' Tiga suggested.

'PLEASE DON'T DO A SPELL, TIGA!' Fluffanora cried.

She'd witnessed many a spell go wrong for Tiga.

There was the time Tiga had tried to brush Mrs Pumpkin, Fluffanora's cat, but had instead just made her completely bald. Mrs Pumpkin was LIVID.

Or the time Tiga had tried to summon an outfit from her wardrobe in Ritzy City to the Cauldron Islands but had instead summoned *the entire wardrobe*. It had hurtled through the sky and squashed her as she stood with her hands raised and eyes closed, waiting for a

dress to neatly slip over her head.

'I just need to think of a spell,' Fluffanora muttered.

'Why don't we try to *carve* a boat out of the broom with our fingernails?' Peggy said, completely panicking.

Tiga threw her hands in the air. 'Leave the magic to me!'

Peggy pulled her hat down lower over her face.

'OK …' Fluffanora said, wincing.

They soared lower and lower. As they got closer to the river, Tiga realised there was nowhere to land. There was a huge drop on either side of the river for miles and miles – there was no way to get close! They would have to do the boat spell in the air and then *land* on the river.

She cracked her knuckles. Her hands were all sweaty. 'OK … here we go …'

They were only seconds away!

'As quick as you can,' Peggy said with an encouraging nudge.

'Right, OK …' Tiga said again.

Her mind was blank!

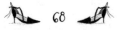

'We're about to die,' Fluffanora said, pointing at the swirling silver water that was only inches away from them now. 'Shall I try a spell?'

'Take this air thing and make it be A SPLASHING AND SWIMMING THING OF THE SEA!' Tiga cried.

There was a bang, and eight human feet appeared on each side of the broom. It plopped into the water.

They wobbled on the broom as the feet flapped about. It was almost identical to a spell Tiga had heard Peggy do at the coves during the Witch Wars competition. A spell that ended, very shortly after Peggy had bewitched a bed to have flapping feet on either side of it, with them sinking.

'At least *this* won't sink,' Peggy said cheerily. 'This broom is much lighter, so it should float. Hopefully. Well done, Tiga.'

Tiga grinned as they swirled around and around, faster and faster towards the glistening Silver City …

WARWOP!

Colour has been seeping back into Ritzy City. Reports of colour elsewhere in Sinkville have also been getting back to us. We have heard of blue grass in the forest, emerald waves in the Cauldron Islands, and apparently Crispy's caravan is fuchsia pink. And so are her eyebrows.

THIS MUST HAVE SOMETHING TO DO WITH SOMETHING BAD AND WE MUST NOT PANIC EVEN THOUGH IT'S PROBABLY CELIA CRAYFISH!

We sought the advice of failed scientist Pelly Peagreen to ask what *she* thinks is causing the colour changes.

Pelly Peagreen: A painter is on the loose!

WARWOP! **interviewer:** Thank you, Pelly Peagreen, for your science.

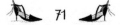

Poor Felicity Bat

'I don't know what Celia Crayfish is talking about, saying you're rubbish. You are really un-rubbish, Fel-Fel,' Aggie Hoof prattled as they soared through the air.

Felicity Bat punched a cloud and carried on levitating.

'Is she everything you hoped she would be?' Aggie Hoof asked. 'Is she, Fel-Fel?'

Felicity Bat ignored her and levitated a bit higher.

Aggie Hoof bounced after her on her mop. 'Fel-Fel, are you sad? You look sad.'

'I'M TRYING TO LEVITATE,' Felicity Bat snapped, turning her head so Aggie Hoof couldn't see the tear rolling down her face.

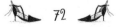

WARWOP!

H OW TO HIDE FROM DANGER! PANICKERS'
EDITION:

- Caves (NOT THE COVES: THE WITCHES
  THERE EAT PEOPLE).
- Wardrobes.
- The Invisible Spell (this only works on non-
  witches. Real witches can still see you, only you
  look like you're wearing a cloud).

As no spells will *technically* protect you from
other witches, who – let's face it – are probably
much better at magic than you ... we've come up
with the Witch Box!

STEPS TO MAKE THE WITCH BOX:

You need:

*A large cardboard box (big enough to cover the
top half of your body).

*A wide-brimmed witch hat.

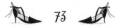

*Scissors (CAREFUL WITH THESE! DON'T PANIC!).
*Some glue.
*Some black paint or black paper (or a big black pen).
*A pair of gloves.
*A magazine with pictures of people's faces (they must look happy and not panicked).

Get the large cardboard box and cut a round hole in the top (big enough to fit your head) add two holes in each side for your arms. Paint the box black, or cover in black paper.

Next, find a picture of a face in a magazine and stick it on to the front with the glue.

Finally, get a wide-brimmed witch hat and cut two holes in the top for you to see out of. Pull the hat down over your face. Put a glove on each hand and get in the box, poking your head out of the top.

THEN NO ONE WILL EVER SEE YOUR SCARED FACE AND WILL THINK YOU ARE A NOT-AT-ALL-TERRIFIED WITCH.

THE WITCH BOX

Oh So Soaked

The water began to slow as Tiga, Peggy and Fluffanora faced a fork in the river – both watery avenues were covered by large silver bridges that glistened in the soft light.

'Which way?' Tiga asked.

Peggy pointed at a sign. 'That way, on the right, leads around Silver City and on to Driptown. This way, the left, takes us straight into Silver City.'

They all leaned to the left, and the mad broom with feet flapping furiously obliged. After a good ten minutes, they were well and truly SOAKED.

As they turned the final corner into Silver City they went under a bridge and found themselves in a glittering silver cave. There were spots to park the boats,

but they were all full. Hundreds of them – silver boats of various shapes and sizes.

The broom glided slowly into an empty space. The cave was eerily quiet and filled with cobwebs. The only sound Tiga could hear was the occasional drip of water into the still pool that surrounded them.

Peggy clambered off, followed by Tiga and Fluffanora.

The ground was smooth and slippery. An old sign pointed towards a tunnel.

'Silver City Town Square (which is actually more of a circle),' Tiga read.

The three of them looked at each other.

'Here we go …' Tiga said, and on they walked, into the dark, dark tunnel …

What a City

'Whoa,' Tiga said as they emerged from the tunnel into the bright light of the city square (or circle). It was completely silent apart from the gentle splash of the fountain in front of them. A large stone witch stood in the middle of it, her arms outstretched. As they got closer, Tiga could see in one of her palms sat a curled-up cat and in the other was a paintbrush with a sparkling tip.

She walked towards it, across the perfect slabs of silver pavement. The place felt warm and comforting, despite being completely empty and covered in cobwebs.

Witches' hats littered the ground.

'Did they all leave for the Big Exit without their hats?' Tiga asked.

Peggy shrugged. 'Maybe they thought they might as well leave them – they'd go all pointy in the pipes and be ruined anyway …'

'I'm sure Miss Heks took her hat … I saw a pointy one in the house once. I thought it was a costume,' Tiga mumbled.

'I think that's the witch who built Silver City,' Fluffanora said as she stood transfixed in front of the fountain. Tiga wiped some cobwebs off the sign.

ALICE BRIGHT: FOUNDING WITCH OF SILVER CITY

(AND ALAN, HER CAT)

SILVER CITY, SINKVILLE'S SECOND LARGEST METROPOLIS, WAS BUILT TO NURTURE GREAT WITCH TALENT. THE TOWN MOTTO IS:
DO STUFF REALLY GOOD.

ALICE BRIGHT BUILT A CITY OF EXCEPTIONAL BEAUTY, A SPARKLING GEM IN SINKVILLE'S RAMBLING LANDSCAPE. THE CITY, AND ALICE

Bright, welcome you silverly (that's the Silver City equivalent of 'warmly').

Thanks for visiting!

Tiga turned around, taking the whole place in. Shops lined the city circle. She walked over to a bookshop called The Silver Stacks, which had lots of copies of *Melissa's Broken Broom* in the window. MEET THE AUTHOR, GLORIA TATTY, read the sign in the window. A witch with silver hair smiled in the photo.

'GLORIA TATTY!' Fluffanora cried. 'I love her.'

'Have you ever met her?' Tiga asked.

Fluffanora shook her head. 'Mum said she came into the shop once when she needed a dress – she was going on a TV show on the Fairy Network called *Scribbles with Fran*. The show didn't last very long – only two episodes, I think. It was meant to be Fran interviewing authors, but Fran just insisted on dressing up as the characters and re-enacting the WHOLE BOOK. And then she did the scene in the book when Melissa bites into the broom and breaks her teeth. She flew around

81

screaming, "My fabulous tooth is chipped!", flew straight into Gloria Tatty and got a leg stuck up each of her nostrils. It took them two days to remove Fran from her face. Imagine having Fran stuck up your nose for two days, poor thing.'

'Poor Fran,' Peggy said.

'Poor Fran?' Fluffanora spluttered. 'Poor Gloria Tatty!'

'Fran will be annoyed we sneaked away to Silver City without her,' Tiga mumbled as she wiped the window of an empty café called Sip. Next to it was a shoe shop called Shoes by Karen, Who Really Struggles to Think of Cool Shop Names.

All the shoes were covered in cobwebs, and Sip was ninety per cent dust.

The shops were flanked by narrow platforms that twisted left and right and led to lots of buildings erected on beautiful sparkly silver stilts.

'Where do we even begin?' Peggy asked.

Tiga grinned. 'Where we know my mum was last seen – at the National Above the Pipes Association, NAPA.'

Fluffanora looked around. 'So we just need to find NAPA … Anyone know what it looks like?'

'I DO,' said a voice, making them all jump.

Tiga gasped.

'It's NORMA MILTON!' Peggy roared, pointing in the air. 'And she can levitate!'

'I learned to levitate a long time ago,' Norma Milton explained. 'It's quite easy, really.'

'It's almost impossible!' Peggy said, completely in awe.

'What are you doing here, Norma?' Tiga asked.

'Oh,' Norma Milton said sweetly. 'I saw you all leaving and thought you might need this for your adventure! I found it in an old shop years ago.'

She produced a map of Silver City.

'This is *exactly* what we need!' Tiga said, hugging Norma Milton. Because she was levitating, she was really just hugging her legs.

Norma Milton giggled sweetly.

'Well,' Fluffanora said, tapping the map with her finger. 'According to this map, NAPA is just across that wobbly platform over there …'

Tiga skipped on ahead. Never had she felt so full of hope, so light and fluttery – *This is what it must feel like to levitate like Felicity Bat!* she thought.

Which was funny, because at that exact moment Felicity Bat was levitating high up above her head.

16
Walk Like a Sleuth

'What are you doing, you little perky pest?'

Fran stopped her mid-air walk and looked at Miss Heks, hiding the book she was carrying behind her back: *How to Walk Like a Sleuth, and Other Useful Walks.*

'Nothing, you big ... monster ... face,' she replied, muttering to herself, 'That was a *pathetic* response, Fran.'

Insults weren't Fran's specialty. She was, however, fantastic at singing underwater, rollerblading and dining with cats.

'Well, get out of here. Go on! Shoo!'

Fran slowly – with the long strides of a sleuth – air-walked past the window as Miss Heks pulled the holey

85

curtains. But it was too late. Fran had already seen the six witches in brightly coloured dresses sitting among the cheese inside. They were all grinning at a particularly green apple …

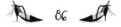

WARWOP!

LOOK! Nottie, the Jam and Cats stall owner let us dress up her cats in lots of little Witch Boxes!

Meanwhile, Back in Silver City...

NAPA Headquarters sat up high on some sparkling silver stilts. A silvery waterfall fell from the bottom of it, but it wasn't water; it was shimmering fabric cut in strips to look like water.

'How do we get up there?' Tiga asked. She couldn't see any stairs ...

Peggy and Fluffanora shrugged.

Norma Milton levitated higher. 'I can help with that!'

Tiga stared at the pool of fabric by her feet. If she half closed her eyes, it almost looked like water. It was familiar somehow. Maybe it reminded her of the time Miss Heks took her swimming (she took her to a puddle and threw her into it), or the time she had spilled

88

a huge pot of cheese water on the floor … Or *maybe* it was familiar because she had been there before, years ago, with her mum …

'Peggy!' Fluffanora squealed, startling Tiga out of her thoughts of puddles and cheese water.

Peggy was halfway up the left stilt, and in true Peggy style, was already completely stuck.

Norma was attempting to lift her, screeching 'Uuuuup! Uuuup!' but was, if anything, just lifting Peggy's skirt up.

'NORMA, YOU'RE MAKING IT *WORSE!*' Fluffanora shouted up to her.

'CAN WE ALL REMAIN CALM! THAT IS AN ORDER FROM THE TOP WITCH OF SINKVILLE!' Peggy shouted down.

'I was wondering when she was going to lord *that* over us,' Fluffanora said with a tut.

Tiga couldn't help but laugh, until Peggy slipped and fell and landed with an almighty thud in the fabric pool below.

'PEEEEEEEGGGGGYYYYY!' she cried.

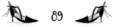

'Can she swim?' Norma fretted as she soared back down towards Tiga. 'CAN. SHE. SWIM? Have we seen her swim? Can she swim?'

'It's *fabric*,' Fluffanora said calmly. 'It's like, I dunno, falling on to some jumpers.'

Tiga bent down and thrust her hand into the streams of fabric.

Nothing.

'PEGGY!' Tiga cried. She couldn't feel anything but the fabric. It seemed to move in her hands, like worms.

'I can't feel her in there!' Tiga cried.

'I can't believe the last thing she did in life was play the I AM THE TOP WITCH OF SINKVILLE card,' Fluffanora said as Tiga slumped over and shakily said, 'I think she's gone.'

'But I am the Top Witch so I'll use it if I want!' Peggy called down.

The three of them slowly looked up. There, dangling out of one of the windows, looking like she was about to fall again, was Peggy.

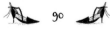

'Dive in,' she said. 'You fall through the fabric and land here, like magic!'

'I think, technically speaking,' Norma Milton said, 'it's definitely done by magic. Not *like* magic. It is magic.'

But Tiga and Fluffanora had already dived in.

Fran Dines with Cats

'Pass the salt,' Fran said to one of the eight cats in Witch Boxes she was dining with. 'I know, I can't believe Tiga would go off somewhere without me either!'

The cat sitting across from her growled.

'My thoughts exactly, cat number two. Oh, I've seen some things, cats. I've seen some things. Celia Crayfish for one, and a bunch of Big Exit witches in Miss Heks's house. I couldn't quite hear what they were saying, but it looked evil …'

'Miaow miaow miaow,' said cat number four.

'That's ridiculous, cat number four,' Fran said, pouring herself some more tea. 'They can't take over Linden House.'

'Miaow miaowmiaow miaowmiaow,' said cat number one.

Fran threw her hands in the air. '*Because* Linden House is protected by magic. It will only let a young witch of nine years old rule.'

'Miaowmiaow,' said cat number four.

Fran shook her head. 'No, it's impossible to over-power magic like that. But you're right, I must find a way to subtly warn all of Sinkville that Celia Crayfish is back. I can't be too obvious or she might come after me! I know, I'll use my extreme fame to slyly warn people about Celia!'

'*Miaow miaow*,' cat number four said again, more pointedly.

'Oh, huge apologies!' Fran said. 'I completely misunderstood you, my cat is not what it used to be! *Yes*, you *can* have the salt.'

Operation Slug

'Whoa,' Tiga said.

Peggy was skipping around some huge models of pipes, which were all lighting up, one by one.

Fluffanora was staring at a poster on the wall with an eyebrow raised.

It was a list of countries above the pipes and their traditional dress.

'Above the pipes is mad,' she eventually said.

Inside, NAPA was vast. They had arrived via some sort of suction chute, Tiga thought – it had all happened so quickly she hadn't really figured out how they got there. One minute she was jumping into the pool of shredded shimmering fabric and the next thing she knew she was being sucked upwards. It was a little like

travelling in the pipes, only not nearly as much of a *smoosh*, much more of a *whoosh*.

The lobby was filled with glowing pipes – they were enchanted, so you could see models of witches moving through them, and the effect pipe travel had on them, in slow motion. In the corner, Tiga spotted a model of floating platforms. They hovered above some fake clouds.

'Sky Ports,' Tiga said, reading the sign out loud. 'The Sky Ports hang above the major Sinkville cities and are used to document pipe activity.'

'Look at this, Tiga,' Peggy shouted.

Peppering the walls were hundreds of posters of above-the-pipes things. Famous kings and queens and rulers and politicians from history, even a list of famous people who were actually witch spies for NAPA!

'Whoa,' Tiga said as she studied the famous-people poster. 'I would've never guessed *she* was a witch …'

'Hey, Tiga!' Fluffanora was pointing at a poster of slugs. 'Come look at this.'

Tiga skipped over and landed with a jump next to her.

OPERATION SLUG

*Gretal Green has been working on ways to
better study the world above the pipes. Ten
slugs were chosen to act as information
gatherers – they have been fitted with new
magic so they can absorb significantly large
quantities of information. Unfortunately,
we haven't quite figured out how to make
them go FASTER.*

Underneath, there was a photograph of each of the ten
slugs. They all looked quite different, which was weird
because slugs look almost exactly the same, until you
look at them *very* closely.

Fluffanora yanked the slug out of Tiga's pocket and
held it up by the tail.

'Hmm,' she said. 'Not that one …' Slowly she moved
the slug past each photo.

'Sluggfrey,' Tiga and Fluffanora said slowly.

'Sluggawhata?' Peggy asked, skidding to a halt next
to them.

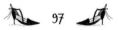

'She's a boy?' Tiga asked, staring at the slug and its massive beehive of Fran-like hair. The slug just blinked at her.

There was no mistaking it – her slug was definitely Sluggfrey. He was smooth and dark grey, with no spots or splodges like the others. Also he had quite big eyeballs.

'We might need to redecorate the doll's house,' Fluffanora said. 'And remove his beehive of hair.'

Tiga was positive Sluggfrey shook his head.

'Fran says that's unisex hair,' Peggy said.

'Wait,' Fluffanora said excitedly. 'Does this mean Sluggfrey is packed with information?!'

Norma Milton shook her head. 'That seems very unlikely. Can I hold the slug?'

Fluffanora prodded him.

Tiga stared at the slug in amazement. 'Perhaps my mum sent him with me. He's definitely hers! He has always been around. He was in the shed the whole time!'

'This is very cool,' Fluffanora said.

98

Lily-Sue
OPERATIVE 1
LOCATION: LOS ANGELES

BELLE
OPERATIVE 2
LOCATION: TOKYO

MARGOT
OPERATIVE 3
LOCATION: TOULOUSE

MAUD
OPERATIVE 4
LOCATION: AMSTERDAM

KLARA
OPERATIVE 5
LOCATION: PRAGUE

CARI
OPERATIVE 6
LOCATION: ISTANBUL

PARI
OPERATIVE 7
LOCATION: TEHRAN

JOSEFINE
OPERATIVE 8
LOCATION: COPENHAGEN

AILBHE
OPERATIVE 9
LOCATION: DUBLIN

SLUGGFREY
OPERATIVE 10
LOCATION: SCOTLAND

'Where do we even BEGIN?' Peggy asked, skipping off ahead down the corridor.

'I guess we should find my mum's office,' Tiga said hesitantly. She wasn't sure what to expect – what she would feel like when she went in and saw her mum's things … What if she got all upset? What if there were signs of a struggle? Something awful? Worst of all, what if they couldn't find *anything* that would help them find her?

She felt something at her side.

'Oh, oops,' Norma Milton said sweetly, slowly lifting her hand out of Tiga's pocket. 'I just *love* your slug.'

Tiga took him out and went to hand him to Norma Milton.

'TIGA, I'VE FOUND IT!' she heard Peggy yell, and she slipped Sluggfrey back in her pocket. She was too distracted to notice Norma Milton scrunch up her fists and whisper, 'RATS.'

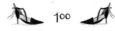

100

Pineapple Face

Back in Brollywood, lights flashed, glittery dust exploded everywhere, the camera zoomed in on Fran.

'HELLO, WITCHES! And welcome to *Cooking for Tiny People* with ME, Fabulous Fran. Today we have a special show that I've just decided to make up myself right now!'

Crispy was behind the camera, smacking her head on it in frustration. The shows were always a disaster when Fran went off script.

'Today … we are going to be cooking a … pineapple. Yes, a pineapple, um, face.'

She flew over to the cupboard and pulled a pineapple out of it.

'First we add some evil eyes.'

She stuck on two grapes, and on to them she put two chocolate buttons.

'Scary eyes!' she said, wiggling about and shaking glittery dust down on to it.

'And a pointy banana nose …'

Crispy was still banging her head on the camera.

'Some fang teeth! I like to use some cut-up bits of apple. But you can use anything as long as you shape it into spiky fangs.'

She flew around the room, ducking in and out of cupboards and chucking things on the floor.

'I'm going to stick some blueberries to the pineapple spikes, so it almost looks like a crown. You know, like old rulers used to wear. And what other kinds of rulers are there? Top Witches. And this *pineapple* is a bit evil-looking, isn't it, IF YOU KNOW WHAT I MEAN? Some might say I'm trying to give you a message. Who else gives messages? *WARWOP* witches, if you know what I mean –'

'What are you *talking* about?' Crispy hissed.

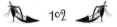

Fran stared at the camera blankly and then held the pineapple high in the air.

'I hope you like this Celia Pineapple, a very excellent BUT DEADLY DANGEROUS recipe that's definitely back in town,' Fran concluded.

'It's not even a recipe!' Crispy said, throwing her hands in the air. 'It's a fruit version of a Mr Potato Head.'

The banana nose fell off.

'And cut,' Crispy said faintly.

Mrs Brew Does Crafting

Mrs Brew chuckled as she watched Fran hold up the pineapple on the screen. She was watching *Cooking for Tiny People* on a large silver spoon.

She looked around her to check no one was there and then flicked her finger. A pineapple appeared, and all the things she needed to make a face. She had almost finished attaching the banana nose when she realised something.

She got to her feet and peered outside. She was sure she spotted something blue and witch-shaped drop from one of the pipes. She rubbed her eyes and looked again. Nothing.

'How peculiar …' Mrs Brew said to the pineapple face. 'You look very familiar …'

She waved a hand and a telephone covered in glittery spiders appeared with a bang. 'Mavis,' she said, holding the phone to her ear.

'Hello, Jam Stall 9, we're here for all your jam, cat and WARWOP needs. Mavis speaking.'

'Mavis,' Mrs Brew said urgently. 'Did you watch *Cooking for Tiny People* today?'

'No, one of the cats ran off with the spoon I like to watch TV on,' Mavis said with a tut.

'Well, I think you should watch it. Mavis, I have a funny feeling Fran was trying to send Sinkville a message …'

Gretal Green's Office

'This is it,' Tiga said.

'I thought that was going to be *much* harder,' Peggy muttered.

There the four of them stood, in front of a sparkling oval door. Above, glowing bold letters spelled out GRETAL GREEN, INVENTOR.

'This is so cool!' Peggy squealed. 'Tiga, isn't this cool?! It's your mum's office!'

Tiga took a step closer to the door and placed a hand on it. She swiftly turned and quickly said, 'I'm not ready to go in there.'

She put her hand in her pocket and felt Sluggfrey snuggle into it.

Peggy patted her on the shoulder. 'There's no rush.'

'Yeah,' Fluffanora said, putting a hand on her other shoulder. 'We have all the time in the world.'

'FEL-FEL, LOOK AT THIS PIPE – IT'S GOT A FAKE WITCH IN IT AND SHE'S GOING ALL WARTY! LOOK!'

'Ssssh, you idiot!'

Tiga, Peggy and Fluffanora stared at each other.

'Who is that?' Norma Milton whispered.

'FEL-FEL, I BET THEY'RE DOWN HERE!'

'You don't want to know!' Tiga said, grabbing Norma Milton's arm and dragging her down the corridor. 'Quick! We have to hide!'

WARWOP!

We imagine you've been too busy panicking to watch *Cooking for Tiny People*, but Mavis of Jam Stall 9 has just been alerted to the fact that Fran has sent us a very important message:

YOU CAN MAKE FACES WITH FRUIT.

Isn't the world amazing?!
   Now, back to panicking.

Amateurs

Fran finished reading the *WARWOP!* article and took a deep breath. 'I am dealing with amateurs,' she said to cat number four. 'I NEED TIGA. *Or* I need to send a more obvious message …'

Invisible Inventions

'OOOH, FEL-FEL, MAYBE THEY'RE HIDING FROM US IN HERE,' Aggie Hoof said, again, TOO LOUDLY.

Felicity Bat shoved her out of the way and read the sign on the door.

'And why, if they were hiding, would they be in the INVISIBLE INVENTIONS ROOM? If they were, then we WOULD SEE THEM BECAUSE THEY'D BE THE ONLY THINGS THAT WEREN'T INVISIBLE!'

'Unless they found an invention in there that made them invisible, Fel-Fel.'

Felicity Bat was flummoxed. Aggie Hoof had made a good point. She had just been outsmarted by Aggie Hoof …

'Fel-Fel? What is happening to your face?'

Felicity Bat held her hands over her ears to stop the steam.

She marched towards Gretal Green's office.

'But that's the most obvious room of them all, Fel-Fel! They wouldn't hide in there. They would know that's where we would look!'

Felicity Bat ignored her and marched on in. Finding Tiga wasn't the reason they were there. Her gran had sent her to fetch something, and that was exactly what she was going to do.

Felicity Bat stopped dead in her tracks.

'Fel-Fel, are you OK?' Aggie Hoof asked.

'Do you think Gran is right? I mean about older people ruling Sinkville, not young witches like us?'

Aggie Hoof stood blinking at her. Felicity Bat *never* asked her opinion on anything.

'Well?' Felicity Bat snapped.

Aggie Hoof thought *really* hard. 'I don't think it matters if she's right. She's evil and that's all that we care about … isn't it?'

Felicity Bat picked at one of her nails nervously. 'But what she's saying is young witches aren't good enough. She thinks we're too stupid to rule Sinkville. Do you believe that?'

Aggie Hoof nodded enthusiastically.

Felicity Bat sighed as she flicked her finger and the door to Gretal Green's office turned to dust.

Fran Sending an Obvious Message

'SHEEEEE'SSSSSS BAAAAAACCCCCCCCCK! BAAAAAAAAACCCCCKKKKKKKKK! SHEEEEE'SSSSS BACCCCCCK! SAW IT WITH MY OWN FABULOUS EYEBALLS. SHEEEEE'SSSS BAAAACCCCK!' Fran squealed as she shot through the town.

'Where?' Mrs Brew yelled after the fretting fairy.

'GULL & CHIP TAVERN, MRS BREW. I LOVE YOU, MRS BREW!'

Mrs Brew charged down the road and straight into the Gull & Chip Tavern.

'OUT,' Nasty Nancy said before Mrs Brew had one full foot through the door. She peered around the room. No Celia Crayfish.

'Is Celia Crayfish back?' Mrs Brew demanded.

Nasty Nancy cackled. 'Oh, you've fallen for the crazi-ness of the WARWOP witches,' she said as she stirred some gloopy Crubbly juice. 'And that hysteri-cal fairy.'

Fran zoomed past the window, doing her professional screaming.

Mrs Brew didn't believe Nasty Nancy for a second. In large part because Nasty Nancy had once written a book called *How to Lie*. She clenched her fists and marched down the road. If those evil witches were back, she was going to find them.

114

WARWOP!

We're pretty sure she's back, everyone. Mainly because Fran has been screaming for hours about it now. So to mark the occasion, we took a break from panicking to compile Celia Crayfish's TOP FIVE BEST MOMENTS from when she was last in Sinkville!

FIVE: That time she turned lots of witches into dolls, which we only actually discovered recently. That's impressively sneaky.

FOUR: That time she started wearing snakes on her waist to look extra terrifying.

THREE: When she appeared on Fran's first ever episode of *Cooking for Tiny People* and actually made a really nice loaf of bread.

TWO: That spell she invented to freeze people and erase their memories. That had lasting damage for a lot of the witches she hit with it.

TWO: That spell she invented to freeze people and erase their memories. That had lasting damage for a lot of the witches she hit with it.

ONE: Winning Witch Wars when she was nine and then being the *worst* ruler Sinkville has ever known.

WE MUST HIDE FROM HER. Especially if she still has that snake ...

Correction: This article has been amended, as since we wrote it, we have been informed that it wasn't actually a snake – it was simply an elaborate belt. Still, it was a scary belt.

Norma Milton Steps Up

'They're going into my mum's office,' Tiga whispered as she peeked along the quiet corridor.

Peggy, Fluffanora and Norma Milton peeked too.

'What are they doing?' Peggy said. 'Are they looking for us?'

'Those meddling pests,' Fluffanora said.

Norma Milton straightened her hat and started walking confidently down the corridor.

'Don't!' Tiga hissed.

'Tiga, it's fine,' Norma said with a reassuring smile. 'They don't know who I am. I'll handle this.'

Tiga looked at Fluffanora, who was shaking her head.

'Don't, Norma!' Peggy said, but it was too late, Norma Milton was already at the doorway.

'Who are you?' they heard Felicity Bat snap.

BANG!

WALLOP!

CRASH!

'She's gone into that room!' they heard Aggie Hoof shout.

'Get her!' Felicity Bat commanded.

'They're chasing Norma down the corridor,' Tiga said, peering around the corner.

'We should get in there while we can!' Fluffanora cried, as the three of them raced to Gretal Green's office.

'And we should save Norma!' Peggy added.

'At some point!' Fluffanora shouted.

'WHOA!' Tiga said when they saw inside the room.

'FROGTOES!' Peggy squealed. 'LOOK AT IT!'

Gretal Green's office was INCREDIBLE. All the walls were covered in weird buttons and levers and a large window wrapped around one side with screens dotted along it. But they weren't blank. When Tiga moved closer, she could see they were moving images. One looked like a beach, with lots of huge feet stomping past. There was one that showed a beautiful iron bridge – Tiga was sure she'd seen it before.

'The Ha'penny Bridge in Dublin!' she cried. 'That's above the pipes.'

'Look!' Peggy cried, wiping some dust off the top of the screen. A little plaque read AILBHE.

Tiga wiped the dust from the beach screen. LILY-SUE.

'I know what it is, it's the slugs!' Fluffanora cheered. 'This must be a live feed of what they can see right now!'

One of the screens was completely blank. It read SLUGGFREY.

Tiga pulled the slug out of her pocket, and just like that, the image in the frame changed to them all standing in the room!

'Cool,' Fluffanora said, moving so close to the slug her face was all smooshed on the screen.

'So at least we know your slug is *definitely* Gretal Green's slug now!' Peggy said, squeezing Tiga's arm.

Tiga looked around the room in amazement. There were weird machines everywhere. One had lots of umbrellas stuck in it, like a large umbrella hedgehog. Tiga flicked a switch and they all shot into the air and began floating around.

Another was a jumble of twisted tubes. When Tiga pressed the big button on the side, it rattled, and out shot what looked like a black-and-white-striped sweet.

' "The Honesty Sweet",' Tiga read. ' "This sweet will always make the eater tell the truth".'

Peggy licked it. 'I'm NICE,' she said.

At the other side of the room, past all the machines and pipes, was a large, messy desk, next to a wall covered in hundreds of levers and buttons. Tiga walked towards it.

The large black chair with glittery silver cushions that sat behind the desk was covered in a thin film

121

of dust. A set of black papers was piled up at one side, and as Tiga got closer, she could see a tipped-over teacup; its spilled liquid had left a ghostly stain on the dark wood.

Peggy and Fluffanora followed behind her.

Tiga slowly picked up a picture on the desk. It was Gretal Green cuddling a baby. They were standing on a platform outside a beautiful silver house that looked out on to the swirling water that surrounded the city. Gretal Green had her face nuzzled into the baby's tiny face and the baby was giggling.

'It's you!' Peggy said, tapping the photo. 'Isn't it?'

'I think so …' Tiga said, staring at it. She'd never seen a picture of herself as a baby. Miss Heks didn't have any photos of her at all.

On the floor next to the desk was a dusty old hat. Tiga picked it up and shook it. There was a thin bow tied around it and it had a sparkly grey edge.

'This must be her hat,' Tiga said, taking off her own and putting her mum's hat on. 'It's the same one she's wearing in the photo.'

Fluffanora gasped. 'And look over here!'

Tiga ran over. Next to the screens mounted on the windows was a board with various pamphlets and papers pinned to it.

HOW TO EXTRACT INFORMATION FROM THE SLUGS, read a bit of paper. But the bottom half had been completely torn off.

Tiga studied it closely. The dust on it had been disturbed. 'This was recently torn off,' she said. 'That evil rat Felicity Bat must've got it! We have to get that piece of paper. Sluggfrey might have important information in him! He might know exactly what happened to my mum ...'

Oh, Hello

'WARNING, WARNING, WARNING!'

'Stop saying "warning", you idiot!' Felicity Bat snapped, hitting Aggie Hoof with the mop.

Norma Milton had somehow managed to suspend them in the air, and they were floating slowly into the office.

'Whoa,' Peggy whispered. 'Norma is better at magic than Felicity Bat …'

'Where did you say you were from again, Norma?' Fluffanora asked, but Norma was too busy concentrating on keeping the two evil witches afloat.

Tiga just stood with her mouth open.

'Yeah, yeah, enjoy it while you can,' Felicity Bat said.

'Put us down!' Aggie Hoof demanded. 'Please?'

Norma cackled.

Tiga pointed at the wall and the torn bit of paper about the slugs. 'Hand it over, Felicity, right now!'

Felicity Bat gasped and shook her head. 'No, it can't be! It can't be!' she cried. 'It was there a minute ago. Do you have it?' she growled, staring at Aggie Hoof.

Aggie Hoof shook her head madly.

Felicity Bat swivelled around, flicked her finger and broke Norma Milton's spell. She grabbed her by the scruff of her neck and lifted her into the air. 'Well, then *you* must have it!'

Norma Milton smiled. 'I don't know what you're talking about.'

'AAAAAAARGH!' Felicity Bat cried, swirling around the room and knocking over inventions left, right and centre.

'Be careful!' Tiga cried. 'And stop lying, we know you have it, Felicity! … Unless you do, Norma?' she whispered.

Norma Milton shook her head. 'I honestly don't.'

Felicity Bat shot out of the window.

'Oh no you don't!' Tiga cried, grabbing a broom and shooting after her.

The cool air outside battered against her face as she tore through the clouds after the evil witch.

Felicity Bat glanced back, saw Tiga and sighed. 'Really, Tiga? You want to fight me?'

'Just give me the piece of paper and I won't attack.'

Felicity Bat let out a cackle that echoed throughout the deserted city.

Tiga just stared at her.

The sound of the swirling silver river was the only thing that filled the silence, and the occasional shout from Aggie Hoof, who was at the NAPA window with Fluffanora, Norma and Peggy, shouting, 'WIN, FEL-FEL! WIIIIIN!'

'Let's not be silly, Tiga,' Felicity Bat finally said. 'I don't have the piece of paper, but neither do you, so I have sort of succeeded in my mission.'

'Your mission?' Tiga asked. 'Did someone send you to get that piece of paper?'

'No,' Felicity Bat said quickly.

Tiga raised an eyebrow and flew around Felicity Bat. 'Who would send you to get that piece of paper, I wonder ...'

'No one,' Felicity Bat said. 'I told you, no one sent me.'

Tiga came to a halt and sighed. 'Look, we don't agree on anything. You are a complete pain, but *please*, all I

want is to know where my mum is, and that slug might know, so I need to know how to get the information out of him, you understand?'

Felicity Bat looked deep in thought, like she was trying to work something out.

'Your mum?' she eventually said. 'What has the slug got to do with your mum?'

Tiga gasped. 'Someone sent you to get the bit of paper … but you have no idea why, do you?'

Felicity Bat cackled and scoffed and crossed her arms defensively. 'Ha! That's ridiculous. I know exactly what I'm doing and why I'm doing it!'

'GET AWAY FROM HEEEEEER!' Norma Milton bellowed at Felicity Bat as she shot through the air, smacking into Tiga and sending her hat flying.

Tiga dived, frantically trying to grab it. It spiralled down and down until *SPLOSH!*

'My mum's hat!' she cried, as she watched it sail off down the silver river.

Norma Milton floated down to her and put a hand

on her shoulder. 'Don't worry, Tiga, it's only a hat. On the plus side, Felicity Bat is gone.'

Putputputputputputput.

'Stupid, faulty, silly-noise-making mop,' Aggie Hoof grumbled as she *putputput*-ed her way through the air above them. 'Wait for me, Fel-Fel!'

Norma Milton patted Tiga again. 'And Aggie Hoof is gone too.'

28

Why?

Felicity Bat peeked her head around the Gull & Chip Tavern door and slowly stepped inside.

'She's not here,' Nasty Nancy said, without looking up from the *WARWOP!* article she was reading.

'Where is she?' Felicity Bat asked.

'Away on important evil business.'

'Right,' Felicity Bat said.

'Ooooh, Fel-Fel, this is lucky. Now you have some time to get that piece of paper about the slugs.'

'You didn't get it?' Nasty Nancy asked. 'Well, that's what we all expected. Further proof that children are useless.'

'I hate to keep reminding you oldies: *you* were once children,' Felicity Bat snapped.

'And then we got some sense,' Nasty Nancy said with a nod.

'Why does my gran want that piece of paper about the slugs?'

Nasty Nancy snorted. 'Not telling. She'd kill me for telling you; she says you're a waste of perfectly good Sinkville space.'

Felicity Bat took a seat at the bar and flicked her finger, setting the *WARWOP!* article on fire.

'Oi! I was readin' that!'

'You're not telling me because you don't know, do you, Nasty Nancy?'

'I know everythin',' she said with a smirk.

'Does my gran need to know what information is in that slug?'

Nasty Nancy cackled. 'Course not, you idiot child. I ain't telling you nothin'.'

Felicity Bat levitated off the barstool and towards the door. 'You just told me everything.'

'Did not,' Nasty Nancy protested.

'Did she, Fel-Fel?' Aggie Hoof asked, trotting after her.

131

'There's only two reasons my gran might want that piece of paper,' Felicity Bat said smugly. 'Either she needs the information in the slug, or she knows it already and needs to make sure no one else gets it. You –' she looked over her shoulder at Nasty Nancy – 'said she doesn't need the information in the slug, so that means she knows exactly what it contains and wants to stop anyone else from finding out what she already knows. And *that* means she thinks the information is something that could ruin everything for her.'

Nasty Nancy stared, mouth open, as Felicity Bat soared out of the door.

'Who's the idiot *now*?' Aggie Hoof said, as she walked into the wall.

Ritzy City?

'FROGNUGGETS!' Tiga cried as they walked down Ritzy Avenue towards Linden House.

It wasn't the same Ritzy Avenue they had left in the middle of the night to go to Silver City. Everything was multicoloured!

Linden House was a gorgeous emerald green, and Brew's was a luscious purple with orange window frames.

Cakes, Pies and That's About It Really was a weird melon colour.

Peggy took off her glasses and rubbed her eyes.

Fluffanora turned on her heel slowly as she walked, trying to take it all in. 'It's like the olden days,' she said suspiciously.

As they passed Brew's, Mrs Brew came shooting out of the door and threw herself at them. She nearly knocked Fluffanora over completely.

'You're back!' she cried. Her cold was gone and she was back to her normal not-snotty self. She straightened up her hat and hoisted Fluffanora in the air, twirling her around.

'How did it go in Silver City?' she whispered.

'We'll tell you all that later. But Felicity Bat was there,' Tiga explained. 'She was on a mission, and I bet Celia Crayfish sent her. I think she might actually be back.'

'That's what the WARWOP witches keep saying. That's how they explain the colour,' Mrs Brew said. 'But no one has actually seen her. Don't tell Fran I said that …'

A spray of glitter smacked Tiga in the face.

'SHE'S BAAAACCCCKKK!' Fran screamed as she zoomed into view.

'Fran!' Tiga cried.

'I think you're forgetting something, Tiga.'

'Fabulous Fran,' Tiga tried again.

Fran nodded and gestured for them to follow her. 'I've seen things since you've been away.'

'Things?' Tiga asked.

'Big Exit witches, back and in town – all colourful.'

'I knew it,' Tiga said. 'I knew Miss Heks couldn't bring all the colour back like this.'

Fran twirled in the air. 'And I saw Celia Crayfish and

135

I have been practising being a detective, and doing an excellent detective walk, like this.'

Fran walked with long, determined strides through the air.

'WHAT?!' Tiga said.

'An excellent detective walk, like this,' Fran repeated, and did the walk again.

'No, no,' Tiga said urgently. 'The bit before. The bit about Celia Crayfish. You *definitely* saw her?'

'Oh yes, she's back. She was in the Gull & Chip Tavern, talking about how she's going to take control of Linden House.'

'I checked the Gull & Chip Tavern, Fran, and she wasn't there …' Mrs Brew said quietly.

'That doesn't mean she wasn't before,' Fran said grandly. 'The WARWOP witches believe me.'

'I believe you too,' Tiga reassured her.

'I should make some sort of official announcement,' Peggy muttered to herself.

'I spied Miss Heks and a bunch of bad witches crowded over a green apple too,' Fran said. 'It was glowing.'

'Like my apple?' Peggy said slowly, before turning and running fast towards Linden House.

Tiga watched as Peggy frantically fiddled with the key and bolted inside.

'What's she doing?' Mrs Brew asked.

Tiga remembered the light switching off in Linden House the night they flew to Silver City, and the figure she was *sure* she saw scuttling across the garden …

'IT'S GONE!' Peggy cried from the window. 'THE GLOWING APPLE IS GONE!'

'I didn't know she was such a fan of fruit,' Fran said. 'If I had known, I would've brought her my Pineapple Face!'

Felicity Bat Overhears Something

'It's horrific. I mean, look at her.'

Felicity Bat was huddled outside the Gull & Chip Tavern. She had been planning to go in but had overheard her gran having a rant to Nasty Nancy about someone and realised it was about her.

'She's just not me,' Celia Crayfish said. 'I don't see any of me in her. SHE'S A DISGRACE. She needs to be destroyed. As soon as I take over Linden House, the first thing I'm going to do is destroy her.'

Felicity Bat shakily got to her feet and vowed that never again would she help her horrible grandmother. *That old bat is on her own*, she thought as she tore off down the road.

In fact, Celia Crayfish was actually talking about the

portrait of herself in the Gull & Chip Tavern, which she felt was not a good or accurate painting of her at all, and she was planning to destroy it.

'Maybe you could get another one painted once you've destroyed that one,' Nasty Nancy said.

'Wonderful idea, Nasty Nancy!' Celia Crayfish cooed.

But Felicity Bat had gone before she could hear that bit …

Felicity Bat
in a Wardrobe

'It feels like something sinister is about to happen,' Tiga said as she watched colour slowly coat the buildings outside.

It was getting late, and one by one, witches strolled up Ritzy Avenue and into the darkness.

Tiga turned back around to face Fluffanora, who – much like her – couldn't imagine sleeping at a time like this.

'I know,' Fluffanora said, as she fluffed the slug's hair. 'Something sinister. You know, I never thought my reaction to a blue cat or a pink pair of curtains or a pavement in a canary yellow would be terror, but it is. I feel like evil witches are hiding everywhere.'

Margaret Mulch, a very evil Big Exit witch who was

hiding in the Brew's attic, heard Fluffanora say that and quietly got up and went to look for a better hiding place.

'Do you hear someone in the attic?' Fluffanora muttered as she put Sluggfrey in his doll's house.

'How are we going to find that piece of paper?' Tiga said with a sigh. 'That trip was a disaster, a dead end. We need to find out what Sluggfrey knows. It's the key to finding my mum, I just know it.'

'We'll find it,' Fluffanora said. 'Hey, did Peggy make her speech?'

Tiga nodded and handed Fluffanora the latest *WARWOP!* article.

'It features me,' Fran said proudly.

WARWOP!

Finally, our most glorious Top Witch has spoken. This is what she said: 'Witches of Sinkville, please do not panic. Yes, colour is seeping back and we do have strong evidence to suggest that it is Celia Crayfish.'

NOTE: AT THIS POINT, A WITCH IN THE CROWD YELLED, 'WHAT EVIDENCE?'

'Well,' Peggy then said. 'A fairy friend of mine told me she saw her.'

NOTE: AT THIS POINT, A LOT OF WITCHES IN THE CROWD STARTED GROANING, 'UGH, FRAN. YOU CAN'T BELIEVE *FRAN*. SHE'S PROBABLY JUST TRYING TO GET HER OWN DOCUMENTARY.'

We spoke to Fran to ask if she was trying to get her own documentary and she said, 'Of course not! I want a *film*.'

142

'Listen,' Peggy went on. 'I am going to get to the bottom of this. I will find Celia Crayfish and speak to her. I am appealing to her now. If she is here and would be willing to come forward and discuss any of her evil plans, I will happily listen to them. Well, not happily, because the plans would be evil and evil plans don't make me happy at all ... *Anyway*, you are all my witches and I will protect you. I will find out what's going on.

'We must remember that Sinkville is magic and so are we. Evil has no place here and must leave right now!'

NOTE: AT THIS POINT, A VERY NICE WITCH CALLED EVIL JONES YELLED, 'OI!'

'In the meantime, I ask you to be vigilant and report anything suspicious to me.'

NOTE: AT THIS POINT, A WITCH IN THE CROWD YELLED THAT ONE OF HER TOENAILS WAS SUSPICIOUSLY LONG.

'The most important thing is not to panic!'

143

> And that's it, fellow WARWOP witches. I think what we can take from Peggy's speech is that WE MUST NOW PANIC.
>
> Yours shakily,
> *The WARWOP Witches*

Tiga put the article down. 'Evil is a really unfortunate first name.'

Fluffanora nodded and yawned.

'Psst,' Fran said, but neither of them heard.

Tiga climbed on to her bed and pulled the covers up to her chin. 'And I lost my mum's hat too.'

Fluffanora took a seat next to her bookshelf and started reading *Melissa's Broken Broom*. 'It's just a hat, Tiga.'

'That's what Norma Milton said.'

'PSSSSST!' Fran hissed in Tiga's ear. 'PSSSSST!'

'WHAT IS IT, FRAN?!'

Fran pointed madly at Tiga's wardrobe. 'There's

144

someone inside, I can hear them.'

'Oh, Fran. You're turning into a paranoid WARWOP witch,' Tiga mumbled sleepily.

Fran floated nervously towards the wardrobe, a hand covering her eyes … She raised a finger, ready to flick it and send the wardrobe door flying off its hinges.

'Oh, I'm going to save you all a lot of bother,' Felicity Bat said as she tumbled out of the wardrobe.

'FELICITY BAT!' Tiga cried.

'Yes,' Felicity Bat said flatly. 'Well done, you have eyes.'

'Aaaaaaargh!' Fluffanora bellowed, throwing herself at the evil witch.

'Can we all just calm down for a second,' Felicity Bat said softly, levitating up so high they couldn't catch her.

'Why must you always be such a menace?' Tiga said, brandishing her fists.

'Why not?' Felicity Bat asked.

Fluffanora grabbed some books off the bookshelf and began pelting them at her.

But Felicity Bat just ducked and dived and shot a couple back at her.

'Look, I know we're not exactly friends,' Felicity Bat began.

'Not exactly, no,' Tiga said.

Felicity Bat levitated a bit lower. 'But I need your help.'

'Our *help*?' Fluffanora spluttered.

'Look,' Felicity Bat said impatiently. 'My grand-mother doesn't know what she's talking about. She came back – they used Miss Heks as a cover. They knew lots of witches would just think the colour is seeping back because of her and not suspect much. While everyone's been debating what it might be and branding the WARWOP witches mad, the Big Exit witches have been sneaking back, one by one. All that colour out there? That's the Big Exit witches coming back.'

'Oooh, I saw them! I saw them! Didn't I see them, Tiga? Felicity, may I interrupt to show you my detective walk?'

Tiga plucked Fran from the air and shoved her in the doll's house. The slug sat on her.

'Rude,' Fran said.

'OK, I'll bite. What do you need help with?' Tiga said.

Felicity Bat levitated even lower. 'They are planning a battle. They expect resistance from other witches. They have matching Evil Witch outfits. Frilly old horrible things from about a hundred years ago.'

'Ruffle-bottom dresses,' Fluffanora said with a knowing nod.

'And she's going to rule Sinkville as an adult and get rid of kid rulers, like the world above the pipes,' Felicity Bat continued.

'How is she going to do that? Only a nine-year-old who has won Witch Wars can rule,' Tiga said.

'Yeah,' Fran shouted from inside the doll's house. 'Linden House is protected by serious magic.'

Felicity Bat stared at Tiga blankly. 'Well, yes, but …'

'That's the bit you need help with, isn't it?' Fluffanora said. 'You have no idea how she's planning to do it.'

'She hasn't told me,' Felicity Bat said defensively, picking at her nails. 'She won't tell me anything!'

'And why don't you want to help her? You *love* her,' Tiga said.

Felicity Bat levitated a bit lower. 'She's going to *destroy* me.'

'Destroy you?' Tiga asked.

'DESTROY ME,' Felicity Bat said again.

'Why do you think we can help you? You're good at spells and levitating and all that stuff – why do you need us?' Tiga asked.

Felicity Bat shrugged. 'You're good. The good guys always seem to win around here these days.'

'How do we know you're not lying?' Tiga asked. 'You lied about having the piece of paper from NAPA, which you *still* haven't given to us.'

'I told you, I don't have it. But I did see it before Norma Milton pranced in and interrupted things. One of you must have it.'

Tiga shook her head. 'None of us would do that.'

'Well then, it was Norma Milton,' Felicity Bat said.

'She's lovely,' Tiga protested. 'She's done nothing but help us – she was the one who gave us a map of Silver City so we could find NAPA!'

150

'Her name is an anagram of "I'm Not Normal",' Felicity Bat said.

Fluffanora burst out laughing. 'Oh my frogs, it is!'

'You're trying to frame her,' Tiga said knowingly. 'This is all so obvious.'

'I'm not,' said Felicity Bat casually. 'You're just going to have to believe me.'

'I never will. Now get out, before I set Fran on you.'

She opened the door to the doll's house.

Fran started rolling up her sleeves and shooting little balls of glittery dust into the air.

Felicity Bat sighed and soared out of the window.

'That was easy,' Tiga mumbled, as she watched Felicity Bat disappear down the street.

Fluffanora joined her at the window. 'You know, I'm almost convinced she was telling the truth …'

'You were just won over by her anagram joke,' Tiga said, rolling her eyes.

Five Minutes Later …

'I AM TELLING YOU THE TRUTH!' Felicity Bat roared, shooting back through the window and startling them all. 'What can I do to prove it to you? Flowers?'

She flicked her fingers and bunches of flowers fell down on them.

Fran was flattened by a bouquet of lovely roses.

'Why you little …' Fran growled through a petal.

'Or … or … chocolates!' Felicity Bat said manically. A load of chocolate boxes from Pearl Peak's chocolate shop, Slopply's Chocolates, shot around the room.

'Stop it!' Tiga yelled. 'Can't you just say sorry for everything you've done?'

Felicity Bat stared at them. Fran looked furious, Tiga looked miffed, Fluffanora looked so amused.

'Oh, right, *that*,' Felicity Bat mumbled. 'Right, yes, please accept this pony as my apology.'

She clicked her fingers and a gigantic horse landed with a thud in front of them. It had one big eye and one really small one, a singed mane and a fang.

'MAKE IT GO AWAY!' Fran cried.

'Hilda?' Felicity Bat said, patting its back. 'She's my horse. What's wrong with her?'

Hilda the horse lifted a spiky hoof and waved it in their direction.

Tiga and Fluffanora took a step backwards. Fran burst out crying.

'Oh,' Felicity Bat said. '… More like this?'

There was a pop and Hilda vanished in a puff of smoke. When she landed back with a thud she was a gigantic fluffy white pony with huge kind eyes.

'What's that supposed to mean?' Fluffanora growled. 'You think because it's fluffy we're going to be like –'

'SO CUUUTTTEEEEE!' Fran cried, zooming towards it and cuddling it. 'So cute, so cute, so cute.'

Felicity Bat shot Fluffanora a *see* face. 'Your name is *Fluff*anora,' she couldn't resist adding.

'I made it up when I was four!' Fluffanora said. 'I LIKE IT.'

'She doesn't really,' Fran whispered in the pony's ear.

Tiga shook her head. 'This is the worst apology of all time. You've come in here with a horse, insulted us – is this what you call a sorry? Just say sorry, Felicity.'

Felicity Bat swallowed hard and looked like she was going to vomit. 'I'm … suuuroorry.'

'You're surory?' Tiga asked. 'S-o-rry. Say it, s-o-rry.'

154

'Sworry.'

'SORRY!' Tiga shouted.

'Sorrrty,' Felicity Bat said.

'SOOOORRRRRRRYYYYY!' Tiga bellowed.

'It's OK! I forgive you!' some random witch from outside shouted.

'Sor–'

'Ry,' Tiga said.

'She can't say sorry,' Fluffanora said, moving closer to Felicity Bat. 'It's *fascinating*.'

'Ssss,' Felicity Bat struggled. 'Ooo.' She gulped. 'Rry.'

The three of them clapped, which is all that's needed to reverse a spell put on a horse, so Hilda morphed back into the scary, singed version with the weird eyes and single fang.

'Baaaaaaah!' Fran cried, before shooting into Sluggfrey's doll's house to hide.

Felicity Bat levitated in the air. 'We have to come up with a plan. We need to stop them before they take over. And for that, we need serious magic. Let's meet somewhere tomorrow morning ... I can teach you a thing or two.'

'Where?' Fluffanora asked.

Felicity Bat shrugged. 'We could meet here?'

Tiga shook her head. 'What if one of the Big Exit witches sees us with you?'

'Good point,' Felicity Bat said. 'We need somewhere hidden. What about somewhere in Silver City? The NAPA magic is really strong and good, according to my gran.'

'Too far,' Fluffanora said. 'We don't have time.'

Felicity Bat began to pace the room. 'We need somewhere close by, where no witch goes ...'

Tiga imagined soaring around Sinkville, stopping at places and scoring them off her list as she went. *Clutterbucks – too crowded. Brew's – too obvious. Cakes, Pies and That's About It Really – too ... delicious.*

'BROLLYWOOD!' Fran bellowed.

'Cameras,' Tiga mumbled in her direction. There was nowhere in the land that she could think of ... and that's when she remembered ...

'I know what to do!' she squealed, jumping up and down on the spot.

Felicity Bat held out a hand as if she was waiting to

receive Tiga's answer like a present. She clicked her fingers. 'Well … say it.'

'The Sky Ports,' Tiga said. 'They were used by NAPA.'

'The Sky whatas?' Fluffanora said.

'Sky Ports. I read about them when we were in Silver City at NAPA. Floating platforms above us in the clouds, hidden from view, remember? The witches at NAPA used them to monitor pipe activity. I'm pretty sure there's one just above Cakes, Pies and That's About It Really. Let's meet there.'

Felicity Bat nodded. 'First thing tomorrow.'

'We'll tell Peggy,' Tiga said.

Felicity Bat bit her nail. 'We could do with some others. What are Lizzie Beast and Patty Pigeon up to?'

Tiga grinned. 'And Milly and Molly?'

Felicity Bat smiled. 'All of us. The Witch Wars witches. We'll stop my ridiculous gran … See you tomorrow.'

'Don't be late!' Fluffanora called after Felicity Bat as she levitated out of the window.

'And don't bring your *pony*!' Fran shouted from the doll's house.

Sky Port

Tiga balanced on a box of carpet cleaner as she, Fluffanora and Peggy (they had chosen brooms) soared up into the clouds in search of the Sky Port. They'd bumped into Norma on the way, so she had joined them. Lizzie Beast and Patty Pigeon were following close behind on feather dusters.

Tiga hadn't had the guts to call Milly and Molly. She was kind of hoping Felicity Bat would …

'It's over here!' Tiga cried.

In front of her, she could see a cloud-shaped platform swaying slightly in the breeze. It looked like it hadn't been used in years – the little station that sat on top of it, which was a bit like a rocket control room, was covered in flaked paint, and the door was hanging off

the hinges. As Tiga got closer, she could see various objects that had dropped down from the pipes on to the platform – old toothbrushes, a sock …

And Aggie Hoof.

'I brought her too,' Felicity Bat said quickly, as she appeared with a pop in front of Tiga.

'Is she on our side?' Tiga asked nervously. To be perfectly honest, she still wasn't even sure if Felicity Bat was on their side …

Felicity Bat cackled.

'Well?' Tiga asked.

'She's my *sidekick*, Tiga. She's on whatever side I'm on.'

Aggie Hoof nodded enthusiastically.

'Right,' Tiga said, as the others caught up with her. Milly and Molly appeared with a pop.

'I told them to be nice,' Aggie Hoof said.

Milly and Molly grinned little fanged grins.

'Everyone,' Peggy said. 'This is Norma Milton. Oh, Patty, you might know her – didn't you say you were from the Towers, Norma?'

'I am, yes! Hello, Patty,' Norma said sweetly.

'I don't remember you at all,' Patty Pigeon peeped.

Felicity Bat clapped her hands. 'NO TIME FOR PLEASANTRIES, WITCHES! Right, we have a gran problem. My gran. I can only apologise. To stop her, we have to hit her where it hurts.'

'IN AN EYEBALL!' Aggie Hoof yelled.

Felicity Bat shook her head. 'No, Aggie, that's violent.'

Tiga watched Aggie Hoof mutter, 'I was sure that was the answer,' to Milly and Molly, who both shook their heads at her in disgust.

'No,' Felicity Bat continued. 'We have to hit her weaknesses. She has three.'

Peggy was frantically scribbling notes in her notepad.

'Her first weakness,' Felicity Bat said, 'is *fire*.'

'Everyone's weakness is fire!' Peggy said, throwing her hands in the air.

Felicity Bat continued. 'Her second weakness is riddles.'

'But she won Witch Wars,' Tiga said, sounding confuddlewumped (a Sinkville term for confused).

'She didn't solve a single riddle in her Witch Wars contest,' Felicity Bat said with a smirk. 'She cheated, got the other witches to solve them and then squashed them all at the last minute!'

'Well I'm confuddlewumped,' Peggy said. 'I thought Celia Crayfish was a genius?'

Felicity Bat shrugged. 'She is, but she can't handle a riddle.'

'What's the third weakness?' Patty Pigeon asked sweetly.

'Tall children,' Felicity Bat said flatly, as everyone turned slowly to look at Lizzie Beast.

She stared down at them and grinned nervously.

'Right, first things first. We brush up on our magic. It's ridiculous none of you can levitate,' Felicity Bat said with a clap of her hands.

☆⭐☆

The next couple of hours were a blur of Felicity Bat being really good at spells and all the others trying to copy her and being terrible.

They tried a freeze spell, which just made Molly's dress explode.

And a melting spell that nearly took Tiga's eye out.

They also practised a spell that makes you invisible, which Patty Pigeon was excellent at.

The last was a levitation class, which ended with Lizzie Beast's head in a pipe and Peggy dangerously close to dying.

'Again!' Felicity Bat cried impatiently, over and over again, until *finally* …

'We're all levitating!' Peggy shouted. 'WE'RE ALL LEVITATING!'

They linked arms and jumped off the platform into the clouds.

'Onwards!' Felicity Bat cried.

'WE'RE WITCH WARS WITCHES!' Tiga cried. 'AND NO ONE MESSES WITH U–'

Fran came soaring through the air and landed in Tiga's mouth.

'Mouth closed, dear, when you're flying. Mouth closed.'

Tiga gagged as she pulled Fran out of her mouth. The other witches cackled.

'She said a couple of days,' Felicity Bat said urgently to Tiga. 'And that was a couple of days ago, so I think she's going to start the takeover soon. Lots of the witches must be back by now. Let's meet back at the Sky Port tomorrow morning. I'll find out what I can in the meantime.'

Tiga nodded. 'Norma?' she said. The witch was heading straight down. 'Are you coming with us?'

'Oh, I'd love to, but I have to meet a friend in Cakes, Pies and That's About It Really. See you tomorrow morning!'

They all waved goodbye, apart from Felicity Bat, who stared back at Norma Milton. She thought there was something very funny about that little girl …

'Do you want to come over to our house for dinner?' Tiga asked Felicity Bat.

Felicity Bat started mumbling awkwardly.

'We'd like you to,' Fluffanora added.

'I've got to go do some ruling,' Peggy said with a sigh before levitating off the platform. 'WITCHES OF SINKVILLE! I'M LEVITATING!'

Felicity Bat laughed.

'I'm going to go home and organise my wardrobe,' Aggie Hoof said.

Lizzie Beast and Patty Pigeon had already made plans to have dinner at Patty's house.

Milly and Molly had sneaked off without saying goodbye.

'What kind of food do you like, Felicity?' Fran asked.

'Oh, you know, old toes, frogs, rats' tails, that sort of thing.'

Tiga, Fluffanora and Fran just blinked at her.

'I'm *kidding*,' Felicity Bat said. 'I eat the same kind of food you do.'

'Are you a fan of *Cooking for Tiny People*?' Fran asked Felicity.

Tiga and Fluffanora stood behind Fran frantically mouthing 'SAY YES'.

'… Yes,' Felicity Bat said.

'Ooooh,' Fran said, hugging Felicity Bat's face. 'I knew I liked you!'

 165

Mrs Brew Stumbles Upon Something

Mrs Brew paced back and forth. 'It's not like them to just disappear without telling me where they're off to,' she said to Mavis, who was making a Witch Box.

'Mmm-hmmm,' Mavis said.

'I've searched everywhere,' Mrs Brew mumbled to herself. She stopped dead in her tracks. There was only one place she hadn't thought to look …

'Back in a minute, Mavis!' she shouted, darting out of the door. She took a few steps and held her breath.

Miss Heks's crumbling old house actually had cheese fumes coming out of the windows.

'Excuse me, Miss Heks,' Mrs Brew said loudly, bursting through the front door.

When she saw what was inside, she SCREAMED.

'Well, hello, Mrs Brew,' Miss Heks said quietly.

Hundreds of multicoloured witches with fang-filled mouths slowly got to their feet.

Mrs Brew backed towards the door as they all advanced on her.

Miss Heks flicked a finger and locked the door. 'What a nice surprise …'

Mrs Brew?

'That's so weird,' Fluffanora said. 'I wonder where she went.'

Mavis sat in the corner, shaking in her Witch Box.

'DID YOU SEE MRS BREW, MAVIS?' Tiga yelled into the box.

Mavis momentarily lifted her hat to reveal her face, muttered, 'No, I've been panicking,' and hid again.

'I'm sure she'll be back soon …' Tiga said, even though she wasn't sure at all.

'Your house is really nice,' Felicity Bat said, looking up the beautiful sweeping staircase. 'My house is nothing like this. Our staircase has bats carved in it, and everything is painted black.'

'Sounds quite cool, in a creepy way,' Fluffanora said.

'What's your mum like?' Tiga asked.

Felicity Bat shrugged. 'She almost never speaks. I imagine that's what happens when you grow up with a horror like my grandmother. I haven't seen my mum in days. When we got word on Pearl Peak that the evil Celia Crayfish might be back, my mum was the first to run.'

Tiga flicked her finger and a huge pile of jam jars landed in front of them. Felicity Bat picked one up and dug a spoon into it.

'I just don't quite understand how she plans to take over Linden House,' Felicity Bat said between munches of jam.

'I know,' Tiga said, licking her spoon. 'Isn't Linden House protected by magic?'

Felicity Bat nodded. 'Only a nine-year-old who's won Witch Wars can rule – and only for nine years. They can hand over power temporarily, but only to another witch of the same age. Strictly no oldies.'

'She must have something up her moth-eaten sleeve,' Fluffanora said.

Felicity Bat got to her feet. 'I'm being of no use, sitting here eating jam with you. I'm going to go find out how my gran plans to take over.' And with that, she dropped the jam jar on the floor, smashing it completely, and soared out of the window.

'She sure knows how to make friends,' Fluffanora said with a smile.

WARWOP!

Dear Fellow Panicking Witches,

AAAAAARRRRRRRGGGGGGHHHHHH!

Hi.

We have it on good authority Celia Crayfish is planning an attack. All witches who want to stop her by panicking should meet at Mavis's jam stall (no cats left). It's stall number 9.

And now, a quick message from our fairy friend Fran:

With a battle on the horizon, the fairies are ordering some new hats! If you would like a specially designed one for the occasion, please simply tick the message you would like on your hat below and then post this bit of paper to Fran at Fairy Five: Set 5, Brollywood, and one of my fairy assistants will take care of it for you.

Fabulous wishes!

Fran x

HAT OPTIONS (please also specify if you'd like fairy-head size or witch-head size):

Fly like a fairy, STING LIKE A BEE.

I heart Fran.

I WILL GLITTER-DUST YOU.

I heart *Cooking for Tiny People*.

TEAM NOT-CELIA.

I Went To a Sinkville Battle and All I Got Was This FABULOUS Hat.

I Want To Be Fran.

Norma Milton?!

'And where have you been, Felicity?' Celia Crayfish said, not looking up from the *Ritzy City Post* she was reading. The front-page story was *WARWOP WITCHES FINALLY PANIC FOR A GOOD REASON: CELIA CRAYFISH ALMOST CERTAINLY BACK ... FAIRIES BUY HATS.*

'There's panic out there, I can smell it with my good nostril,' she said with a smile. 'Where's your idiot sidekick?'

'She's organising her shoes in order of heel height,' Felicity Bat said. 'Where's Miss Eggweena Heks, *your* sidekick?'

'Organising her cheese in order of stink.'

Felicity Bat nodded sympathetically.

'Um … Granny, Your Royal Evilness,' she asked. 'How are you going to seize power tomorrow *exactly*?'

Celia Crayfsh took off her reading glasses and got to her feet. 'Felicity, that is something you don't deserve to know. Not unless you have that piece of paper for me?'

Felicity Bat looked guiltily at her shoes.

'Thought not.'

'I … I tried really hard to get it, but I was just, well, there was a girl there called Norma Milton and she was quite good at spells and she … she overpowered me.'

Celia Crayfsh rolled her eyes. 'You shouldn't have been messing around in there. You should've got Norma Milton under control with a stun spell or something, not chased her down the corridor with your silly sidekick.'

'I was trying really hard to – WAIT A MINUTE,' Felicity Bat said. 'How do *you* know we chased Norma Milton down the corridor?'

Celia Crayfsh stared at her, then rolled back her sleeve. 'My all-seeing watch, of course.'

'*No* …' Felicity Bat said. 'That watch is well and truly broken.'

Felicity Bat took a step backwards. 'And you have the glowing apple. A little helper got it for you, you said.' She gasped. 'Norma Milton is helping you?'

It all happened too quickly for Felicity Bat to do anything about it. In a flash, Celia Crayfish darted across the room, flicked her finger, and a cage landed around Felicity Bat. She held her finger up to her mouth and flicked it again. 'Never mess with the best, Felicity.'

Felicity Bat grabbed frantically at her mouth, but no matter how loudly she shouted, no words came out.

'And no, it's worse than that.' Celia Crayfish twirled around and with a bang was transformed into Norma Milton. 'I *am* Norma Milton, and I've seen everything that you've been up to, Felicity. All your BETRAYALS and mess-ups. But now your meddling stops.'

Felicity Bat rattled the cage, but it was no good. It rose up and up and finally attached itself to the ceiling, making Felicity Bat look like a really weird light fixture.

'Do you like my new find?' Celia Crayfish/Norma

Milton said, waving the ripped piece of paper about the slugs in the air.

Felicity Bat shook her head in disbelief. She watched her gran shove the piece of paper in her pocket and head for the door.

'Now,' said Celia Crayfish/Norma Milton, 'if you don't mind me, I have some friends to meet ...'

She flung the door open and skipped outside. But as she did, a little gust of wind whipped the piece of paper out of her pocket. It floated softly to the ground, right below the cage where Felicity Bat was trapped.

Felicity flicked her finger over and over again, but her magic wasn't working. All she could do was stare at it.

Up Here!

However, the next day …

'Morning, Fel-Fel! Time for another day of not knowing how evil or good we're going to be!'

Aggie Hoof trotted into the Gull & Chip Tavern and looked around. 'Fel-Fel?'

Nasty Nancy was snoring on the counter, but aside from her, it was empty.

Felicity Bat rocked in the cage and shook it, desperately trying to make some noise, but Aggie Hoof was humming the song 'Frogs For Ever' by the Silver Rats and couldn't hear.

She turned to leave and Felicity Bat slumped in the cage. *But*, right before Aggie Hoof trotted out of the door, Felicity Bat watched as she turned quickly and

spotted something! Not Felicity Bat in the cage, the idiot. No, she spotted the piece of paper!

'Oooh, maybe this is the slug paper that everyone's been going on about. Because … it has pictures of slugs on it … and it's paper!'

She picked it up, kissed it, and into her pocket it went …

Felicity Bat sighed with relief. At least the paper wasn't in Celia Crayfish's hands. But, then again, maybe hapless Hoof having it would be even worse …

Felicity Bat Isn't Going To Show

M eanwhile at the Sky Port ...

'She's tricked us!' Tiga said, peering over the edge of the platform into the clumps of clouds below.

'That evil witch!' Fluffanora said, stomping about on the platform.

Peggy shook her head. 'I really thought she was telling the truth ...'

'Curse her and her quite good "I'm Not Normal" anagram,' Tiga shouted.

Norma Milton beamed like she was proud. 'She figured that out, did she?'

Tiga wasn't paying attention. 'Why would she trick us? What do you think she was doing? We could've put ourselves in grave danger trusting her.'

'Ah, graves,' Norma Milton said affectionately. 'I love a good grave.'

'What?' Tiga asked.

Norma Milton smiled. 'Nothing …'

'Fel-Fel?' came a voice through the clouds. 'FEL-FEL?!'

'Aggie Hoof,' Tiga hissed.

She came wobbling into view on her old mop. 'Hi, everyone.'

Everyone glared at her. She slipped, sending her mop spinning. She tried to steady herself. 'Have you seen Fel-Fel?'

'Maybe she knows something,' Fran whispered.

'I say we get rid of her,' Norma Milton said, raising a finger, ready to flick her with magic. 'Let's not listen to anything she says.'

'Where is Felicity Bat?' Tiga demanded, squeezing Norma's finger to stop her doing a spell.

'I don't know, silly! That's what I just asked you!' Aggie Hoof said cheerily. 'I've looked all over for her. I said I would meet her in the Gull & Chip Tavern, but she isn't there.'

Tiga began to pace with Peggy.

'I think she's telling the truth,' Peggy whispered. 'She's terrible at lying. Watch this.'

Peggy walked over to Aggie Hoof and asked, 'Is Celia Crayfish back?'

Aggie Hoof puffed out her cheeks, 'Are you meant to know she's back or not? I've forgotten …'

'See,' Peggy said.

'Anyway,' Aggie Hoof said. 'I'd better go check Pearl Peak for her.' She waved goodbye, with what at first looked like a hanky in her hand.

As her mop started to take off, Tiga grabbed it and dragged her back down again. 'What's that?' she asked.

'Oh, this?' Aggie Hoof said casually. 'It's a piece of paper about slugs that Fel-Fel really wanted when we visited Silver City. I *just* found it!'

Norma Milton frantically rummaged in her pockets and then began to choke.

'Are you all right, Norma?' Fluffanora asked, slapping her back.

'Fine,' Norma said breathlessly, staring in horror at the piece of paper.

'May I borrow it?' Tiga asked Aggie Hoof.

She nodded. 'You can take it for now if you want. But only if you promise to look after it for Fel-Fel?'

Tiga held the piece of paper in the air and grinned. Shakily, she took the slug out of her pocket. This was it! She was going to find out what had happened to her

mum. Nothing else mattered. The training. Hideous Celia Crayfish. What on earth Felicity Bat was up to. All that could wait.

Peggy and Fluffanora put a hand on her shoulder and Fran plonked herself down on her head.

Tiga gently took off the slug's beehive of hair with a wave of her hand.

Sluggfrey looked furious.

Tiga's hand was shaking as she read out the instructions.

'OK, so now we tap his head and repeat the following:

Spy slug, spy slug
Slimy and slow
Show us what it is
You –'

BOOM!

Tiga dived to the floor. Sluggfrey soared high into the air. Cackles rang loudly in Tiga's ears – so loudly she clutched her ears in pain.

'WHAT'S GOING ON?!' she screamed.

Peggy and Fluffanora were lying next to her, clutching their ears too.

'This must be it! The beginning of Celia Crayfish's evil plan! RUN!' Norma Milton cried, sneakily trying to grab the slug.

A siren sounded. Colourful witches swarmed the streets below, cackling like a cackle machine that had a broken 'off' button.

Fluffanora and Peggy looked at Tiga, their eyes wide. 'EVIL WITCHES,' they all yelled at once.

SMACK!

Millbug-Mae, the fairy with oversized eyeballs, hit the platform and swirled about in the air. She was wearing a cap that said *Fight Like a Fairy, Sting Like a Bead*.

(She had meant *bee*, but when she called up to order the hats, the witch on the other end of the line had misheard her.)

Tiga watched as all the fairies, including Crispy, tore through the air towards the evil witches. Fran sped off

to the front to lead the way. She whipped out a hat and placed it on top of her beehive of hair, only it didn't say *Fight Like a Fairy, Sting Like a Bead*, it said *Fran's Army*.

The other fairies scrunched up their fists and waved them at Fran.

'Come along, fabulous army!' she said grandly.

Witches were filing down from Pearl Peak too, and witches soared across from the coves, and the towers.

Tiga watched as people ran for cover and closed curtains and dived into plant pots.

A bunch of WARWOP witches waddled past in Witch Boxes.

'WHAT DO YOU MEAN STING LIKE A *BEAD*?' witches were yelling at the fairies. 'WHAT DOES THAT EVEN *MEAN*?!'

'Do beads sting?' another asked, ripping off her beaded necklace and hurling it through the air. It hit Crispy. Tiga watched in horror as the evil-looking little fairy hit the pavement and was squashed under a fleeing witch's sparkly shoe.

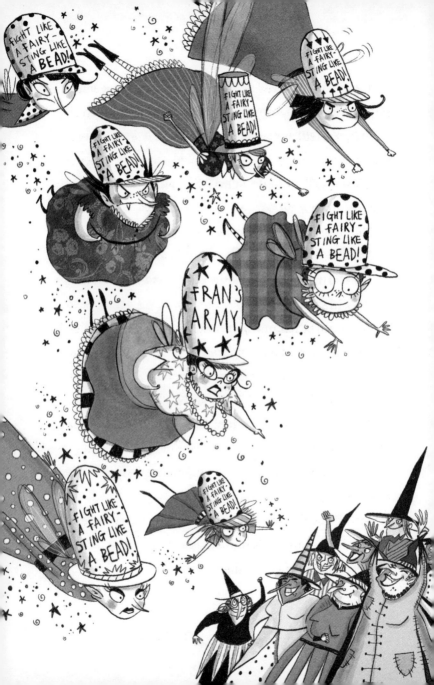

'Crispy!' Tiga cried. The fairy might have seemed evil, but Tiga was positive she was just misunderstood.

Crispy lay still for a moment and then leapt to her feet, squished her face about a bit and looked as good as new.

'I'VE GOT TO DO SOMETHING!' Peggy cried, looking down at all the destruction.

Fluffanora nodded. 'But we need a plan. We can't just run down.'

'SERIOUSLY,' a witch screeched, 'HOW DO YOU STING LIKE A BEAD?'

This wasn't their normal battle. There were no fairies with cameras, no lights, no glitter, no Felicity Bat and her silly sidekick. This was terrifying, and they were not prepared *at all*.

'OK,' Fluffanora said numbly, 'this is it. I'll take on Miss Heks. She's Celia Crayfish's loyal sidekick – we get rid of her, we get rid of a big support for that evil old witch.'

'And I'll deal with the army of evil Big Exit witches,' Peggy said, as hundreds scuttled past below them.

'And I'll look after the slug!' Norma cried.

Tiga turned and peered over the platform. Through the clouds she could hear screams and screeches. 'And I'll deal with Celia Crayfish.' She handed the slug to Norma. 'When you get a chance, do the spell and find out what information is in him. The rest of us will take on the other witches.'

Norma nodded obediently.

'You lot, come with me. You can help me get to Celia Crayfish,' Tiga said, pointing at Milly, Molly, Patty Pigeon and Lizzie Beast. 'Keep an eye out for Felicity Bat too. I want to know what that sneak is up to.'

They all nodded, and off they went, levitating off the platform and down to the, quite frankly, lunacy below.

'Well, that was outrageously easy,' Norma Milton cackled as she watched them go. With a bang she morphed back into Celia Crayfish. She held the slug at arm's length away from her and grinned.

Fluffanora vs Miss Heks

Fluffanora crept along the road behind Miss Heks, who had broken off from the rest of the Big Exit witches and was causing havoc all on her own.

'You!' she bellowed, pointing at Cakes, Pies and That's About It Really. 'Are a lump of BRIE.'

She flicked her finger and the shop transformed into a gigantic lump of cheese.

'Yum,' she said, trotting on further down the road. The lamp post morphed into a stinking lump of blue cheese with a flick of her knobbly finger, and Clutterbucks was soon a fragrant Camembert cheese.

Miss Heks walked up to it and licked it.

Fluffanora gagged.

'You're Cheddar,' Miss Heks said dismissively,

flicking her finger and turning Brew's to cheese. A bunch of nice witches who had been hiding inside ran out holding their noses.

When they got to the end of the road, they were engulfed by a group of Big Exit witches.

Fluffanora gulped, just as Miss Heks twirled on her heel and spotted her. 'Yooou,' she seethed.

'Stop cheesing everything, you horror!'

Miss Heks cackled. Fluffanora flicked her finger. Miss Heks ducked and cackled some more.

Fluffanora stepped forward just as the blue cheese lamp post flopped over. She dived backwards, but by the time she'd got back on her feet, Miss Heks was gone.

'Frognuggets,' Fluffanora muttered under her breath as she watched Miss Heks soar off towards Linden House.

Peggy vs All the Other Big Exit Witches (She Chose It)

'Um …' Peggy muttered as she landed with a thump in the middle of the Big Exit witches. Slowly, they closed in on her.

'The ruling witch,' one of them hissed, grabbing for her.

'Wait!' Peggy cried. 'Let's just talk.'

They paused and tilted their heads.

'Yes?' Peggy begged.

They cackled and lunged for her.

'PEGGY!' Fluffanora cried as she raced down the street.

The Big Exit witches swarmed like wasps in ruffle-bottom dresses. Fluffanora couldn't see Peggy or hear her. The cackles grew louder. Fluffanora glanced around

for Tiga. Cakes, Pies and That's About It Really, now a pile of Brie, was melting.

Milly and Molly scuttled into the scene and pinched Nasty Nancy's nose.

Nasty Nancy just pulled it off.

Peggy gasped as Nasty Nancy pulled another nose out of her pocket and stuck it on her face. 'I got plenty of noses. Is that all you witches have?'

Milly and Molly ran away.

Peggy could see Lizzie Beast and Patty Pigeon in the distance – evil witches were hitting them with bits of cheese.

Think, Peggy, Peggy thought.

Nasty Nancy dived for Fluffanora!

Peggy squeezed her eyes shut, her mind a blender of words and panicking and muddled-up spells.

And then …

POP!

She peeked with one eye and then another.

'Peggy!' Fluffanora cried. 'You're a genius!'

The Big Exit witches had flopped over and were

193

scuttling haphazardly around Peggy, who had muttered in her panic to remember spells:

'*Um … um … Take these evil things and make*
*   them be*
Splashing and swimming things of the sea.'

'Brilliant,' Fluffanora said, shaking her head. She darted forward and opened the door to Brew's.

'Why is it made of cheese?!' Peggy squealed.

'No time to explain!' Fluffanora shouted. 'Herd the witches in here!'

'You brats! Why do I have eight feet!' one witch yelled as the eight feet now attached to her sides scuttled left and then right before heading into Brew's.

'IT DOESN'T MATTER WHAT YOU DO TO THEM,' they heard a voice shout.

'Celia Crayfish,' Peggy gasped, pointing to the roof of Linden House, where the old bat was hovering.

'YOU'LL NEVER STOP ME NOW.'

'Where on Sinkville's grey earth is Tiga?' Fluffanora said, frantically looking up and down the street.

Peggy stared up at Linden House and gasped. 'There,' she said, pointing a trembling finger.

Tiga vs Celia Crayfish

'You have *got* to be quiet,' Tiga hissed, as she levitated slowly up the side of Linden House. Next to her was Fran and all the other fairies who were whisper-chanting, '*Sting like a bead, sting like a bead.*'

It was not ideal.

'Almost there,' Fran said as they wobbled through the air, and came to a halt right in front of Celia Crayfish. She was standing on the roof holding a glowing apple and grinning like Fran on International Fran Day (only Fran celebrates it, on 29th March).

She was drunk on power.

'I AM SO POWERFUL!' she cried, before spotting Tiga staring at her. Fran stuck her tongue out at Celia Crayfish. The other fairies copied.

'Oh,' Celia Crayfish said. '*You.*'

Tiga landed with a thud on the roof and said, 'Yes, *ME,*' before instantly regretting it because it sounded stupid.

She glanced around the roof. It was just her, Celia Crayfish and the fairies.

Tiga took a couple of steps backwards. The wind was picking up and Celia Crayfish, like the apple, was starting to glow.

'You see, Tiga. Your mum was a very clever young witch. She bewitched some slugs to hold information.'

Tiga nodded and turned to her left. Two figures were tied up in the darkness.

'Mrs Brew!' Tiga shouted. 'Mavis!'

They both wriggled. Celia Crayfish had gagged their mouths with some silky gloves from Brew's.

'Ah yes, I thought Mrs Brew could live here and make all my clothes when I'm Top Witch and Mavis can make the jam.'

That must be why Felicity Bat was being nice to us – she was distracting us while her horrible gran kidnapped

Mrs Brew, and Mavis too! Tiga thought. She clenched her fists and made to run at Celia Crayfish, but her legs were glued to the roof! She stared down at them and screamed.

'You don't think I would've thought of that?' Celia Crayfish said with a smirk, gesturing at Tiga's legs. 'I think of *everything*.'

Tiga could hear a scratching noise behind her. She peeked to her right and saw Peggy and Fluffanora levitating by the side of the building.

Fluffanora held a finger to her lips. Tiga nodded.

'Anyway,' Celia Crayfish went on. 'A bunch of us left to live above the pipes. Oh, it was splendid. We made children cry and made potions with toes again, just like the wonder years. We took our houses and marvelled at the world above the pipes and how children are considered inferior to adults. You'd hear people say things like, "I know best!" and do you know why they said they knew best?'

'Yes,' Tiga said.

'Course you do, you were raised above the pipes. IT'S

BECAUSE THEY WERE OLDER. Older than the little runt they were speaking to. But after some years, we got a bit fed up of that world up there – all the sneaking around and the lack of cauldrons. Let me tell you, people look at you very strangely if you tell them you need to buy a bath to make your "soups". We decided to come back.'

'We wanted our Sinkville back,' Miss Heks shouted from Brew's.

'But there was no way we were going to let a kid tell us what to do!' Celia Crayfish said with a cackle. 'I tossed and turned night after night, trying to think about how we could seize power, I wanted to take over Linden House, but the magic that protects it prevented me from doing so. You have to be nine. And I am a bit older than ten.'

'You're a fossil!' someone from the crowd shouted.

'And then one night Miss Heks over there called. She was complaining about *you*, and about how you'd been spending hours in the shed talking nonsense to a slug.'

'From sunrise to frogs o' clock,' Miss Heks said with a sigh.

'And *that's* when I remembered my conversation with your mum,' Celia Crayfish said, smirking. 'You see, I visited her once and she told me about how she'd bewitched the slugs to absorb information. So I bewitched this apple here, you see, just like your mum did with the slugs, only this apple, thanks to a few

tweaks, doesn't just absorb information, it absorbs *youth*. The youth of the ruling witch. So all I needed to do was make sure Peggy held it in her hand, and she did. So now when I hold it, the magic surrounding Linden House can't tell me and the apple apart. So it thinks I'm nine,' she concluded, sounding delighted with herself.

'You *hacked* magic?' Tiga asked.

'*Exactly*,' Celia Crayfish said with a twirl.

Tiga peered over the roof and watched as witches fought and buildings of cheese toppled over, splattering in the streets. There was Lizzie Beast struggling to close the cheese door to Brew's on Nasty Nancy, who had *a lot* of feet, while Patty Pigeon stood next to them yelling, 'Just be NICE!' And Milly and Molly were racing around with the cove witches rounding up the evil witches like cattle, and Aggie Hoof was holding her nose wading about in some cheese. They were all there, apart from two people … Norma Milton, who Tiga hoped was getting the information out of the slug on the Sky Port as they spoke – it was their only hope – and one other …

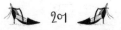

'Where's Felicity Bat?' Tiga said to herself.

Celia Crayfish rolled her eyes. 'Oh, that brat. She's not participating in today's events.'

'She's your granddaughter …' Tiga said.

'She's a DISGRACE,' Celia Crayfish snapped.

Tiga's mind was racing. If Felicity Bat was telling the truth about her grandmother being horrible to her, then maybe something bad had happened to her and that's why she didn't make it to the Sky Port. Tiga felt awful.

Celia Crayfish gazed at the apple and giggled. It was a familiar giggle to Tiga, but she couldn't quite place it …

Celia Crayfish skipped to the edge of the roof and that was when everything clicked into place.

Norma Milton appeared at the same time the rumours about Celia Crayfish started. Norma Milton insisted on being involved in everything. She had an old map of Silver City. She was there when the slug paper went missing and Felicity Bat was insistent she didn't have it. She took the slug for safekeeping … No one knew her

or had met her before. It was almost like … she wasn't really … real …

Tiga gasped!

All the fairies turned and looked at her.

'*What?*' Fluffanora hissed from the side of the roof.

'*YOU'RE* NORMA MILTON!' Tiga roared at Celia Crayfish.

'What?' Peggy whispered.

Celia Crayfish snaked towards Tiga, giggling. With a bang she was instantly transformed into the little girl, and then back to her stringy old self again.

Peggy slapped her hand to her face.

'I'm Not Normal,' Fluffanora said knowingly.

Tiga grinned a triumphant grin, but stopped when she saw what was in Celia Crayfish's pocket.

'SLUGGFREY!' she cried.

The little slug stared helplessly at her.

Tiga could feel her legs wobbling. She leaned forward and tried to grab Sluggfrey, but with her feet stuck she just wasn't close enough.

The fairies all started talking fast to each other, clearly trying to plan an attack because every so often you'd hear 'ATTACK'.

ZAAAAP!

The fairies hurtled to the ground as Celia Crayfish blew gently on her finger. 'Easy,' she said with a cackle.

Tiga peeked over the edge nervously, with one eye open. She sighed with relief when she saw Fran waving a fist from the ground where she and her fellow flying things were *completely* crumpled.

'Ha!' Fran said. 'You may have crumpled our wings but our bones are fine!'

'I think my foot has come off …' Tiga heard Crispy grumble.

'Well, without wings *they* are out of action,' Celia Crayfish said with a cackle. 'Now what are you going to do?'

'What does Sluggfrey kno–' Tiga stopped and fell quiet.

'Oh, I love watching the hope drain out of people,'

Celia Crayfish giggled, jumping up and down in front of Tiga.

Something terrible had just occurred to Tiga. If Norma Milton had actually been Celia Crayfish in disguise, then she would've seen that Felicity Bat was actually on Tiga's side, on the good side. Which could only mean …

'WHAT HAVE YOU DONE WITH FELICITY BAT?' Tiga demanded.

Celia Crayfish's hat nearly slid off her head as she cackled even louder than before.

'Oh, don't pretend you care, Tiga. I took care of her, the witchy little double agent. She's locked away somewhere nice and secure.'

Tiga glanced back down at the crumpled fairies on the ground. All of them were there, but Fran was hurriedly dusting off her skirt. She looked at Tiga and winked.

'Fran?' Tiga said quietly, as she watched the tiny thing fly wonkily off up the street and into the distance.

'Where's she going?' Tiga said to herself, completely

forgetting Peggy and Fluffanora were hanging off the
edge of the roof, hiding.

'Probably to get her hair done,' Fluffanora whispered
back.

Flying Fran

'Eeeeeeeeeeeeeeeeeeeee!' Fran squealed as she shot through the air. 'Eeeeeeeeeeeeeeeeeeeeeeeeeeeeeeeeeeeeeeee!'

Fire

'Wait,' Tiga said. She had an idea. 'You are the most talented, powerful witch in Sinkville, correct?'

Celia Crayfish bowed her head and smiled. 'Correct.'

'Well, then you should give us a chance to beat you. Three chances, that's all we ask for.'

Celia Crayfish shrugged. 'Fine. Pick your first contender.'

Tiga whistled. Milly and Molly looked up. 'I choose the twins Milly and Molly.'

They stood outside the door of Linden House looking up at Celia Crayfish on the roof.

'Remember what we talked about – the *three* weaknesses,' Tiga hissed.

Milly had already flicked her finger before Tiga could finish.

A pretty fireplace filled with roaring flames appeared beside Celia Crayfish.

Tiga put her head in her hands.

'What is *this*?' Celia Crayfish scoffed. She flicked her finger and a stick of marshmallows appeared with a bang. She began roasting them on the fire. 'You're going to have to do better than that.'

And Some More

'Eeeeeeeeeeeeeeeeeeeeeeeeeeeeeeeeeeeeeeee!'
Fran was still flying, squealing 'Eee'.

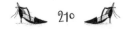

Rude

'FOR THE LOVE OF A FROG IN A HAMMOCK,
STOP SQUEALING EEE!' a witch hiding behind
a plant pot screamed in the air.

Riddles

'I nominate Patty Pigeon!' Tiga cried.

Patty shyly stepped forward. She'd done the invisible spell, but as the WARWOP witches explained earlier, all witches can still see you if you do the invisible spell, it just looks like you're wearing a cloud …

'Remember the three things,' Tiga said to Patty, her eyes wide.

Patty nodded.

'I … I am real but you can't really see me. I'm light but heavy – what am I?'

'You're Patty Pigeon doing an invisibility spell,' Celia Crayfish said flatly.

'FROGNUGGETS!' Tiga cried.

212

And Some More

'Eeeeeeeeeeeeeeeeeeeee,' squealed Fran, now mainly just to annoy the rude witch hiding behind the plant pot. 'Eeeeeeeeeeeeeeeeeee.'

She was almost there.

Tall Children

Lizzie Beast stepped forward.

Celia Crayfish looked queasy. She tried to look at Lizzie Beast but then turned away.

'Isn't she *tall*,' Tiga oozed.

Celia Crayfish swayed like she was going to faint … 'Such a tall … child,' she croaked. She stumbled backwards. Lizzie Beast just stood there, confused.

'It's working,' Tiga whispered excitedly, but then …

BOOM!

In the distance was an almighty noise as glitter exploded everywhere.

'Fran!' Tiga howled. 'ALWAYS WITH THE GLITTER!'

The commotion startled Celia Crayfish out of her weird trance. 'AAAAAARGH!' she yelled, flicking her finger and sending Lizzie Beast flying. 'I win.'

Fabulous Tracking

Fran was pleased with the BOOM! she made as she shattered the locked door to the Gull & Chip Tavern. *Good use of glitter*, she thought. She had stopped eee-ing and was instead patting herself on the head, saying, 'Fabulous tracking, Fran. Fabulous.' She looked up at the cage hanging from the ceiling of the Gull & Chip Tavern.

She shot some glitter into Felicity Bat's mouth. 'POW!'

'*Fran, finally,*' she said, wiping some dust off her tongue. 'Grandmother put a spell on me.'

'Time to get you out of heeeeeeeeeeere!' Fran cried, racing towards the cage in a flurry of wonky wings and glitter.

Felicity Bat covered her face and ducked.

Beetles

Celia Crayfish sent sprays of beetles showering down on the crowd below. They squealed and ran for cover.

'This is going to be too easy, Tiga,' she said.

Tiga desperately tried to flick her finger, but nothing was happening. She watched helplessly as Celia Crayfish took a step forward and bellowed, 'WITCHES OF SINKVILLE, this is my official acceptance speech. I am your ruler now. No longer will the Top Witch be a *child*. Children are useless beasts who shouldn't be trusted with anything, let alone where to put a lamp post or how to regulate Sinkels. Oh, up above the pipes it is simply GLORIOUS. The children up there, they don't have power, they have *homework*!'

She cackled and turned to Tiga, who was only half listening – she'd been distracted by a witch-sized glitter-covered thing levitating its way up Ritzy Avenue.

'GRANDMOTHER!' the glitter-covered thing shouted. 'STOP!'

Celia Crayfish nearly dropped the apple in shock. 'Felicity,' she stammered. 'What are you doing here? And why are you *sparkling*?'

Felicity Bat glared at Fran, who shrugged and muttered, 'The glitter was necessary.'

'You'll never stop me!' Celia Crayfish cackled. 'None of you can – you're just children!'

Felicity Bat shot through the air and tried to grab Celia Crayfish, but the old bat flicked a wrinkly finger, and before Tiga could blink, Felicity Bat was spiralling down into the beetle-covered crowd below.

'Noooooooooo!' Tiga cried.

She looked frantically from Celia Crayfish to the crowd.

'Now that my official speech is over, Tiga, you can stay stuck here as a reminder never to mess with me.'

Tiga whimpered.

Celia Crayfish stuck her nose in the air and said grandly, 'I think it's time I took my rightful place on the Top Witch throne.'

'Oh, they got rid of that,' a witch in the crowd shouted. 'Big Sue melted it down to make a new statue.' She pointed across the street to a beautiful statue of Pat the Chef cuddling a spoon.

'Arrrrrrgh!' Celia Crayfish bellowed before zapping it with her finger and smashing it to pieces.

Tiga frantically tried to unstick her feet. She couldn't see where Felicity Bat had gone. Peggy was hanging precariously by one hand from the roof – she could only levitate for short bursts. Fluffanora had darted across the roof and was desperately trying to untie Mrs Brew. Fran was trying to iron out her crinkled wings.

Tiga looked from them to Celia Crayfish. The apple in the evil witch's hand was glowing really brightly now. She climbed up on to the chimney and dangled a foot over it. 'Like Santa does,' she said quietly.

Tiga turned to Peggy and shouted, 'The apple!'

Peggy nodded, heaved herself on to the roof and batted Fran through the air towards it.

'NO SWATTING!' Fran roared as she somersaulted around and around, up and up. All eyes in the crowd followed her and everyone instantly felt sick.

They held their breath, until …

Splam (it's like a splat but less intense).

'YAAAAAAYY! WOOOOOOOO! GOOOOOO FRAAAAAAAN!'

The crowd went wild!

Fran turned around and waved adoringly at them as she clung on to the apple.

Celia Crayfish, completely bamboozled by the whole thing, regained her composure and began furiously trying to shake Fran off.

'Oh no you don't!' Felicity Bat yelled, rising up from the crowd and zapping her grandmother. The evil thing froze; only her eyes and mouth were moving. Her mouth was shouting, 'RAAAAAATS!' and her eyes looked like they were saying, 'MEGA RAAAAAAATS.'

'Whoa,' Tiga said quietly.

And then ...

CRUNCH.

Crunch. Crunch. Crunch.

Crunch. Crunch. Crunch. Crunch.

Fran gulped down the last bit of apple and wiped her mouth. The crowd cheered. She held the stalk up to Celia Crayfish's face, paused, and then SNAPPED IT.

'NOOOOOOOOO!' Celia Crayfish cried.

A beautiful cage appeared around her.

She rattled the bars and madly flicked her finger but she couldn't get out.

'Remove this cage at once! Who did this?'

Felicity Bat stepped forward. 'You could say I learned from the best.'

Celia Crayfish's mouth fell open.

The crowd cheered.

'Let me out, sweetie dearest,' Celia Crayfish said.

'Let us out too, sweetie dearest,' came Miss Heks's muffled voice from inside Brew's.

'GRANDMOTHER,' Felicity Bat said, standing tall. 'You are *completely* out of control.'

Tiga, Peggy, Fluffanora, Aggie Hoof and Felicity Bat linked arms.

'WAIT FOR US!' a voice bellowed.

Lizzie Beast linked arms with Tiga, and Patty Pigeon linked arms with her.

'AND US!' a couple of squeaky voices said.

'Milly and Molly!' Tiga cried, as the terrible twins joined the chain.

Together the nine of them stood, staring at Celia Crayfish.

'This is our world and it's time you left,' Felicity Bat said.

'Oh, sweet little children, thinking you know best,' Celia Crayfish said with a cackle.

'We do know best,' Tiga said.

'And we've won,' Felicity Bat said flatly.

'You're like old fruit – all spoiled. But you won't spoil us!' Patty Pigeon said, in what was a very insightful, if unexpected, outburst.

'We're great fruits,' Lizzie Beast said, taking the fruit analogy a step too far.

Milly and Molly nodded furiously.

'I've prepared something special for you all,' Felicity Bat said, tossing the broken apple stalk into the cage with Celia Crayfish. 'Somewhere you can live for ever. BUT WITH NO MORE MAGIC BECAUSE YOU ARE IRRESPONSIBLE OLD TOADS.'

Slowly Celia Crayfish rose up and up in her cage and disappeared with a CLANG into one of the pipes.

There was a pleasant little POOF noise and all the other evil witches vanished too. Extra feet and all.

Sluggfrey's Brain

'Well, that was pretty impressive,' Fluffanora said, high-fiving Felicity Bat.

'Where did you send them?' Peggy asked.

Felicity Bat grinned. 'Oh, nowhere *too* terrible.'

'Now we just need to find out what Sluggfrey knows!' Tiga cheered.

'FROGS RIDING ON TURNIPS! I COM-PLETELY FORGOT ABOUT SLUGGFREY!' Peggy cried.

'Do frogs ride turnips?' Fran mumbled.

No one was listening.

'Here's Sluggfrey,' Fluffanora said, handing Tiga the slug.

Tiga was sure he was giving her a 'That was CLOSE'

look, but she couldn't be sure, because his face was slimy and generally expressionless.

Fluffanora placed Sluggfrey gently on the ground and Tiga put a finger on his head.

'*Spy slug, spy slug,*
Slimy and slow
Show us what it is
You KNOW.'

Instantly, Sluggfrey began to shake.

'He's not going to explode, is he?!' Tiga cried.

Fluffanora held her back. 'We need to find out what he knows.'

Out of his head shot a huge hologram of a globe. It was a globe of the world above the pipes. It spun around and around, flashing lights across the countries, and then it stopped.

London.

The countries on the globe vanished and it turned translucent, like a crystal ball.

It was Sluggfrey's view of the shed. Fran was there! She was chatting to Tiga! She made Tiga's name rearrange itself into 'I AM A BIG WITCH'.

'Good times,' Fran said with a sigh.

'But this is really recent,' Tiga said.

Fluffanora took out the piece of paper and studied it.

'Ah, if you want to rewind, you have to push his left eyeball.'

'Sorry, Sluggfrey,' Tiga whispered as she stuck a finger on his eyeball.

The image began to rewind. Faster and faster. Back to Tiga's adventures with the slug in the shed. Then to Miss Heks dancing romantically with a piece of cheese. She kissed it.

'Ewww,' Aggie Hoof said.

Backwards it went some more.

'Speed it up by keeping your finger on the eyeball,' Fluffanora said.

'So sorry, Sluggfrey,' Tiga mouthed as she held her finger to the eyeball.

It was moving fast now.

'STOP!' Peggy cried. 'This is it.'

They all crowded around. There the evil witches were. Miss Heks and Celia Crayfish. It was dark outside. Gretal Green was sitting slumped at her desk reading something. A single lamp illuminated her hands as she turned the page. Tiga could see the Eddy Eggby doll propped up against her mum's book.

Miss Heks was wandering around the office, accidentally knocking things over and picking them up again.

Gretal Green eyed her nervously. 'You're asking some very strange questions, Miss … what did you say your name was?'

Celia Crayfish sat in the chair in front of Gretal Green's desk, her hands clasped neatly in front of her. She had a wig on and a gigantic hat, but it was still definitely her.

'Pam,' Celia Crayfish said. 'My name is Pam.'

'Pam,' Gretal Green repeated.

'Pam. So the houses, how can we move them through the pipes?' Celia Crayfish asked.

Gretal Green shook her head. 'Like I said earlier, I cannot help you with that. Why are you going up there anyway?'

'Holiday,' Celia Crayfish said dismissively.

'Not to torture children?'

'Nope.'

Celia Crayfish ran her hand across the table and

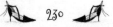

stroked the slug, briefly blocking the camera's view. 'And the colour, how do we stop that from switching to black and grey? We'd like to be in colour up there.'

'You can't stop the colour from changing. Our spells here at NAPA mean you will always be in black and white up there, and colour down here.'

'Not if we devised a spell to *steal* Sinkville's colour and take it with us,' Celia Crayfish muttered to herself.

'Why would you ever want to do that?! That would mean everything would be in black and white down here! I would find a way to stop that!' Gretal Green got to her feet and shakily raised a finger. 'You are up to something, I know it.'

Celia Crayfish picked up the slug and dangled it in front of her face.

'Eww,' Fran said, wincing as they got a view right up Celia Crayfish's nose.

'What's the slug for?' Celia Crayfish asked.

Gretal Green took a seat back at her desk. 'It's a new absorbing spell we invented. The slug absorbs lots of information about the world above the pipes.'

'Have you been doing any evil magic?' Celia Crayfish asked.

Miss Heks, who was still marching about the room fiddling with buttons and levers, snorted.

'We prevent *evil* magic,' Gretal Green said.

'Yes, well, in my day, you could turn a witch into a doll and no one would bat an eyelash,' Celia Crayfish said, snatching the Eddy Eggby doll and putting her in her bag.

'Oi! That's my doll,' Gretal Green cried. 'Get out of here, leave! I shall be reporting you, *Pam*, to the Top Witch.'

Celia Crayfish flicked her finger and momentarily froze Gretal Green.

Felicity Bat tapped the screen. 'That's her freeze spell – erases the memory, usually back about twenty-four hours, but sometimes more depending on the witch.'

Celia Crayfish strolled over to a lever on the wall, yanked it and then snapped it in half.

Tiga gasped! The whole crowd watching gasped! When Celia Crayfish moved the lever, Gretal Green had vanished. Only her hat was left!

'You know,' Felicity Bat said excitedly, 'those levers in NAPA were new security levers they were working on. When you flip them they launch a safety measure and hide you – in this case it sucks you into your hat. It probably sucked everyone in Silver City and everyone else within range into their hats. My gran and Miss Heks must have done a spell to stop themselves from being sucked into their hats too. I read something about the levers when I was in your mum's office – they hadn't perfected them yet. But the levers are designed to snap back after about ten minutes, otherwise you'd be stuck like that for ever. But this lever obviously didn't in all the years between then and now … because my gran broke it. They must have planned all this.'

The slug view moved and peered at a baby in a basket next to Gretal Green's desk. It was Tiga! Her chubby fingers reached out for the slug.

'Lucky you weren't wearing a hat, Tiga,' Fluffanora said.

'Get that slug, Eggweena,' Celia Crayfish snapped at Miss Heks. 'It might've absorbed all of this, and we can't have anyone knowing what we did to poor little Gretal

233

Green.' She peered out of the window at the thousands of hats that littered the empty streets of Silver City and beyond. 'And all of Silver City and beyond,' she said with a snort, before stalking out of the door.

'Well, I guess you must be the slug …' Miss Heks mumbled, staring strangely at the baby and completely missing the actual slug.

She grabbed the baby's basket and turned to leave. The slug wriggled furiously and fell, off the desk and into the basket.

'Sluggfrey wriggled his way into your basket!' Peggy cheered.

Miss Heks looked down into the baby's basket and whispered, 'Time for you to leave Sinkville.' She began to sing, 'We're going above the pipes and we're going to scare some children …'

'So wait,' Fluffanora said. 'Celia Crayfish went above the pipes to terrify children, like everyone suspected, but she didn't take your mum with her –'

'She somehow sucked your mum into a hat?' Peggy said. 'Sinkville is a minefield of silly magic, isn't it?'

'That means the Big Exit wasn't nearly as big as everyone thought,' Fluffanora mused. 'Most of the witches were sucked into their own hats. Only the really evil ones left Sinkville. That's why we saw so many hats in Silver City!'

'Well, this is just BRILLIANT!' Felicity Bat squealed in uncharacteristic glee. 'All we have to do is fix the lever, flip it and then your mum and everyone else who vanished will pop back out of their hats!'

'This is great!' Peggy said. 'She's not dead or kidnapped or melted or anything, she's just in her hat! … Tiga?'

'Tiga?' Peggy said again.

Tiga sat in the corner with her head in her hands. 'I put the hat on.'

'What?' Felicity Bat asked.

'I was wearing the hat when we were arguing outside NAPA. I dropped the hat in the river, remember? She's … gone.'

'DUN, DUN DUUUUN,' Fran said, being completely inappropriate.

 235

Bad Witches
Above the Pipes

'I mean, of all the places to be banished to with no magic for ever, this isn't half bad!' Miss Heks said, putting on her hairnet and staring adoringly around the cheese factory.

Celia Crayfish and her band of evil witches SCREAMED.

Ready!

'Ready?' Felicity Bat said, levitating up to Fran's flying
level.

'REEEEAAAADDDDDYYYYY!' Fran roared,
attaching the camera to her head. She hadn't worn it
since Witch Wars and she was giddy about it.

The plan was for Felicity Bat to fly to Silver City (she
was the quickest) and fix and flip the lever, all while Fran
filmed it for everyone to see, just like in Witch Wars.

Felicity Bat had been so brilliant throughout the
whole battle, teaching them how to levitate and helping
to defeat Celia Crayfish, that Peggy had asked her to
come and help her rule at Linden House. As long as she
promised not to be evil.

Tiga was still curled up in a ball in the corner. As

much as she was delighted that all the Silver City witches would be back after being stuck in their hats for ages, with her mum's hat lost somewhere in the river, she knew she was never going to find her.

'WAIT!' Tiga cried, leaping to her feet.

'That's the spirit,' Peggy said, slapping her on the back.

'No, no, no,' Tiga said urgently. 'What if you flip the lever and Mum is at the bottom of the river and drowns or something?'

'Or she'll swim to the top?' Felicity Bat said, clearly loving all the attention from the hundreds of witches gathered around her and not keen to abandon the mission.

'Why don't you follow after us, and hover above the river on a broom?' Fran suggested. 'That way, if her head pops up you'll see it!'

Tiga threw her hands in the air. 'Really? That's all you've got?'

'That is really all she's got,' Felicity Bat said, as Fran tapped her head, presumably attempting to knock some more ideas out of it.

'All right,' Tiga said. 'I'll be right behind you.'

The Cart Witch

'You havin' a bad day? Why not make it better with GENUINE HATS WOT GOT STUCK IN THE PIPES!' the old cart witch said with a toothless grin.

'No, thanks ...' Tiga grumbled.

All the witches were gathered around a big screen. On it, Felicity Bat was soaring through the sky towards Silver City. She wasn't far now. Tiga grabbed a broom.

'I'd better go, but I'm never going to find her,' she said, to no one in particular.

'I'll come with you,' Fluffanora said. 'Oh, and cart witch, I understand your prophecy now! It makes sense.

'An elegant witch will rule this land,
And that bossy one will lend a hand.

Witch sisters, maybe, but not the same.
One is dear.
The other? A PAIN.
And, much like the tales of times gone by,
They will find a sweet apple and ... My oh my, is that
    the time? I'd better go.'

'It all makes sense now,' Tiga said. 'Felicity is the
pain.'

'Is Peggy ... elegant, though?' Aggie Hoof asked. 'She
doesn't even have a nice dress.'

They all turned and watched Peggy doing some of
her classic 'dancing'. She was throwing her hands all
over the place and bumping into people. Her hat was
lopsided and her dress was ripped.

'Who said it had anything to do with what she *looks*
like?' the old cart witch scoffed. 'Course she's elegant.
Terrible dancer. Maybe the worst in all of Sinkville ...
But her behaviour, her words – nothing but elegant.'

She turned to Aggie Hoof. 'Stop worrying about
what people look like, it's nonsense, unlike

GENUINE WITCH HATS WOT GOT STUCK IN THE PIPES!'

Aggie Hoof thought about it for a moment and then grabbed a mouldy old hat from the cart and put it on her head.

Tiga gasped.

'It's actually not that bad, Tiga,' Aggie Hoof said, gagging slightly.

'No, no, no!' Tiga said, jumping and pointing at the cart.

Under the mouldy hat was one that was a little less battered, but nevertheless completely soaked in silvery water.

'MY MUM'S HAT!' Tiga roared.

'Technically,' Fluffanora said, 'I think it's actually your *mum*.'

The Lever

'One!' the hundreds of witches gathered around the screen yelled.

'Two!'

On the screen, Felicity Bat fiddled with the lever.

'THREE!'

Felicity Bat pulled it! Fran turned the camera round on herself and squealed with delight.

'Turn the camera around! We can't see!' witches yelled.

'We want to see Felicity!'

'What's happening?!' squealed the witches, as Fran pranced about in front of the camera.

None of them knew it yet, but all across Silver City, Driptown and beyond, witches were popping out of discarded hats.

'THAT FAIRY IS OUT OF CONTROL!' a witch yelled, as Fran began what would be an elaborate routine on rollerblades made out of biscuits, with large sparkly buttons for wheels.

Fluffanora and Mrs Brew turned around. There, staring at each other by the carts, was a once-lost NAPA witch, her daughter and a very special little slug …

'Tiga?' Gretal Green said, her voice all squeaky because she hadn't used it in years. 'Oh, Tiga!' she squeaked again, scooping her up and squeezing her tightly.

All the witches in town winced as Fran shimmied across the screen. 'A one, two, three, a one, two, three …'

Tiga buried her head deep in her mum's shoulder. She peeked out in time to see Sluggfrey wink at her.

'I knew you'd find me,' Gretal Green whispered, just as Fran yelled, 'LEEEEEEG KICK!'

'Someone turn it off,' a witch in the crowd pleaded, and the screen with dancing Fran vanished.

'I'LL NEVER ACCIDENTALLY GET SUCKED INTO A HAT EVER AGAIN, I PROMISE,' Gretal Green rambled as she twirled Tiga around and around.

Tiga grinned like she'd never grinned before. It was a grin to rival Fran's grinning at award ceremonies (and those grins were something to behold).

'AND I'LL NEVER BE MISTAKEN FOR A SLUG AND STOLEN EVER AGAIN!' Tiga said as Gretal Green looked confused.

The entire crowd turned quickly to face Tiga and her mum.

Mavis flicked her finger and a bag of popcorn appeared in her hand. 'Now *this* is entertainment.'

Another witch in the crowd dabbed her tear-soaked eyes with a hanky. 'Oh, it's just wonderful!'

Tiga and Gretal Green turned awkwardly to the audience of witches slowly, at the exact same time, scrunching up their faces in the exact same way.

Party

All across Sinkville, in its capital Ritzy City and the once-empty cities and towns beyond, witches danced and sang and drank Clutterbucks.

'Trilly's Tea?' Mrs Clutterbuck asked Tiga, thrusting a pretty little cup into her hand. 'Some say you can see the future in it.'

'Oh you can! You can!' Mrs Clutterbucks' long-lost sisters chirped.

Tiga stared down into her cup and saw only an image of a hoover. 'I think mine is broken,' she mumbled.

Gretal Green swung Tiga around and into the crowd, where everyone danced up and down the streets. Tiga smiled as her mum danced around and giggled, twirling her, Peggy and Fluffanora in turn.

Peggy paused, wiped her brow and then levitated high up above the crowd and squeezed Fran, sending a burst of glittery dust into the air like a firework.

'If I could have everyone's attention, please!' she said.

Everyone fell silent.

'WE DID IT, DIDN'T WE?!'

The crowd cheered.

'SINKVILLE IS EXCELLENT ONCE AGAIN!'

The crowd went wild!

'I have two announcements to make. Firstly, none of this would've been possible without the amazing efforts of everyone here, and to honour the occasion, I have created a statue in the form of one very special person involved.'

'I hope you got my measurements right,' Tiga heard Fran say.

'And that person is one very special slug!'

Fran gasped as a tiny statue of a slug was revealed.

The crowd went wild!

SLUGGFREY

Tiga stared down at Sluggfrey nestled in her pocket. She was sure he was delighted, but it's impossible to tell with a slug.

(Two days later Fran would stick a picture of her face on the statue and pretend it was actually a statue of her. They do have the same hair, after all …)

'And secondly, I have decided to appoint someone to help me rule over Sinkville, as some of you might have already heard. An advisor. Someone very talented who can teach me a thing or two.'

Peggy smiled at the crowd.

'Please put your hands together for FELICITY BAT!'

Felicity Bat levitated next to Peggy and hugged her as everyone clapped.

'Any evil nonsense and you're out,' Peggy whispered.

'Any of your dancing and I will run willingly,' Felicity Bat said, nudging her. And they both erupted into fits of cackles.

WARWOP!

We were right about Celia Crayfish! WE WERE RIGHT. She *was* back. We finally panicked for a good reason!

We would like to take this opportunity to apologise to the cats of Sinkville for the following articles; we were wrong:

- CATS CAN HOLD FORKS – DON'T BELIEVE THEIR LIES
- CATS ARE GREMLINS IN FURRY COATS
- DO YOU REALLY KNOW WHAT YOUR CAT IS THINKING?
- CAN CATS FLY? AND OTHER VITAL SECURITY QUESTIONS

57

The End

Tiga's mum whistled and a silver hoover with pipes sticking out of each side fell from the sky with a thud. Resting on the pipes were cushions. One on each side.

'One for you, one for me,' Gretal Green said with a smile as she hoisted Tiga on to it.

She placed Sluggfrey on a tiny extra pipe and flicked her finger. A cushion appeared underneath him.

Tiga held on to the handle and waved as the hoover took off.

Below her, all her Sinkville friends waved up at her.

'Bye!' Tiga cried. 'But not for ever!'

'Until tomorrow,' Mavis called after her. 'You can come back and help clean up some of the cheese!'

The crowd laughed and Tiga laughed too. 'I'll see you all tomorrow!'

'Bye, Tiga!' Peggy said with a frantic wave. 'I'll get the Sinkville Express train back up and running so it's really easy to get from Ritzy City to Silver City!'

Tiga smiled down at her and off she, Gretal Green and Sluggfrey went, soaring into the darkness.

Gretal Green wrapped her coat around Tiga.

'Where to?' the robotic hoover asked.

'HOME!' Gretal Green said.

Tiga snuggled into her and sighed.

She was in the middle of thinking, *This is magi-* when a burst of glittery dust erupted around them like fireworks, nearly knocking them all out of the air!

'It's ME!' Fran said as she hugged the back of Tiga's head. 'I thought you might need a hand settling into your new city. And who better to help you than me. I am fabulous, you know.'

'I know,' Tiga said.

'And I am *your* fairy,' Fran said with a grin. 'Although

don't tell my fans. They wouldn't like me having a favourite …'

'Of course,' Tiga said with a smile.

'Oh, that would be terribly upsetting for them. *Terribly*. Could you imagine the uproar? Fran has a favourite and it's not me! Oh no, no, no, we couldn't have that! Could you imagine, Gretal Green? Oh, and did you see how I styled Sluggfrey's hair? What do you think? Oh, I love being part of the Green family! I really add something, I think. Don't you? … Oh, you're concentrating on driving the hoover. That's fine. Oooh, shall we sing a *song*?'

A WITCH WARS ADVENTURE

Read on for a peek at
the next WITCH WARS adventure

AVAILABLE NOW!

A New Life in Silver City
(Also Dennis)

Has there been anyone
more fabulous, ever?
Nopedy nope!
Fran, Fran, for ever!

'I'm never going to get that song out of my head,' Tiga groaned. 'And I haven't seen Fran for *weeks*.'

'It really sticks, doesn't it? I woke up singing it,' Gretal Green said as she poured a silvery liquid into a tiny teapot. It was being held in the middle of the table by a lean arm clad in a beautiful lace glove.

'Is that … a real witch's arm in that glove?' Tiga asked, wincing as it swivelled to face her.

Ever since she'd arrived in Silver City, Tiga had

had so many questions, like why did everyone foot-wave instead of hand-wave when saying hello? Why did Winglecca, the witch who owned the cinema, refuse to speak to anyone apart from the sparkly bat statue outside the door? And what was the silver liquid everyone drank every morning? And that was before she got started on her mum's weird inventions. She got the impression her mum was both admired and feared in the town – a genius who could potentially fix their every problem, but might also accidentally maim them all.

'No, no, that glove is one of my inventions, Tiga!' her mother said, twirling around the gleaming black kitchen with all the momentum of someone acting in a musical. 'I got it out of the attic just for you! It's just a bewitched glove. I call him Dennis.'

'Dennis?'

'Yes, Tiga. Dennis.'

Dennis scooped up the teapot and swivelled around, pouring it efficiently into a little puddle on the floor next to Tiga.

Tiga looked from the puddle to her mum, who was rubbing her chin.

'Never quite gets the distance right …' she mumbled, as Tiga flicked her finger and the liquid leapt obediently back into the teapot.

'You're getting very good at spells,' Gretal Green beamed.

A dress danced into the room, making Tiga jump.

'WHAT IS THAT?!'

'Another invention,' Gretal Green said proudly.

'Let me guess, it's called … Gertrude?'

'No, he's also Dennis.'

'WHAT?' Tiga cried.

'Well, I made an entire outfit, and all the parts are called Dennis.'

There was stomping coming from the attic.

'Dennis the shoes were out of control, so I locked them in the attic. Dennis the tights ran away …'

Dennis the dress floated through the air, a frilly monstrosity of lace and ribbons. It wrapped around Tiga. 'That's a hug,' Gretal Green explained.

Tiga watched as her pet slug, Sluggfrey, slimed his way across the table. He was joined by a couple of his fellow slugs, Ailbhe and Clara. When Tiga found her mum, she also discovered one of her mum's experiments – a bunch of slugs that were sent above the pipes to spy on non-witches. They all lived in the doll's house in the hallway. All ten of them.

Who else had breakfast with pet slugs and various items of frilly bewitched clothing called Dennis?

'We're not normal witches, are we?' Tiga said.

Gretal Green cackled. 'Who wants to be a *normal* witch?'

'Me,' Tiga said quietly to herself.

'GOOD MORNING, FANS *SLASH* FAMILY!' Fran the fabulous fairy squealed as she glided into the room, shooting glittery dust everywhere. 'Isn't this wonderful! I'm visiting! And just in time for a family breakfast.'

Tiga smiled and waved at Fran as Dennis the dress turned and headed for the door. Dennis the glove leapt off the table and grabbed hold of Dennis the dress, and the pair of them disappeared into the hallway.

'Rude,' Fran said with a snort. 'That is not how you treat THE *MOST FABULOUS* FAIRY SINKVILLE HAS EVER SEEN.'

'Certainly not,' Gretal Green said with a smile. 'It's lovely to see you, Fran! Look at all the wonderful glittery dust you've brought with you!'

Fran bowed as Tiga ducked under the table and scraped some glittery dust off her tongue.

'Everyone loves glittery dust,' Fran said. 'And everyone loves me.'

'Glittery dust …' Gretal Green said quietly as Tiga resurfaced from under the table, coughing. 'That gives me an idea …'

'An idea?' Tiga said nervously.

'What's for breakfast, servant – I mean, Gretal Green?' Fran said, clicking her fingers.

'Oh,' Gretal Green said, completely lost in thought. Her eyebrows knitted like they always did when she was mulling over a new invention. Tiga tensed at the thought of what her mum would come up with next. 'What would you like, Fran?'

'Jam,' Fran demanded.

'Absolutely,' Gretal Green said, waving her hand. 'We haven't had jam since we returned, have we, Tiga?'

Tiga shook her head meekly, wondering why her mum was waving her hands.

Fran wasn't paying attention. 'Shall we sing my song "Fran, Fran, For Ever"?'

'No,' Tiga and Gretal Green said quickly as a pot of jam with long ostrich-like legs came stalking into the room.

'Another invention?' Tiga asked.

Gretal Green shook her head. 'No, the legs came free with the jam.'

Fran looked unimpressed as the jam jar leapt on to the table and smashed. Tiga looked down at the disgusting mouldy black goo.

'Ah, yes,' Gretal Green said quietly. 'I forgot I've been trapped in a hat for years. I'll need to buy some new jam.'

Fran began licking the table. 'What?' she asked, spotting Tiga's scrunched-up face. 'Aged jam is a delicacy. Probably.'

Dennis the dress came floating back into the room, a frilly arm outstretched in the direction of the jam.

'No, I will not share my fine aged jam with a … dress thing,' Fran scoffed, flopping her entire body on the table and spreading out in a starfish shape, completely covering the jam. 'Especially not a *frumpy* one.'

Dennis the dress floated on the spot.

'Shoo,' Fran said, slapping the frilly sleeve.

Tiga watched as Fran lapped up the jam. It reminded her of the weird goo Peggy'd had on her hair when she first met her. *I'm Peggy Pigwiggle. I like your mad clothes – you must be from above the pipes* echoed her friend's chirpy voice from the box in her brain filled with memories.

'Tiga?' Gretal Green asked. 'Are you all right?'

'YOU CAN'T HAVE MY JAM,' Fran said, aggressively gobbling it.

'I'm fine,' Tiga mumbled, though she wasn't really. She missed Peggy and Fluffanora and Mavis with her stall of fresh jam. She hadn't seen them in weeks; she'd been too busy settling into Silver City, getting to know her mum. She had everything she'd ever dreamed of in Silver City, apart from one thing: she didn't have her friends. She wondered what Peggy and Fluffanora were up to at that very second. *Probably having a breakfast of fresh Mavis jam, curled up on the floor of Linden House together, laughing about something*, she thought.

'TOO MUCH!' Fran roared, rolling off the table. 'I'M GOING TO BURST.'

LAVISH TIGHTS
WANTED
IN CONNECTION WITH
ROBBERY AT SILVERS,
THE GEM SHOP,
APPARENTLY

Olivia Opal, owner of Silvers, insists the robbery committed this morning at her gem shop was the work of 'a lavish pair of tights'.

Made with fine silk gauze and patterned with delicate lace, the tights trotted in and started robbing, using one leg like an arm to scoop the gems from the counter, and the other as a sort of sack.

We spoke to Olivia Opal, who said she had reported the incident to Top Witch Peggy Pigwiggle in Ritzy City.

Witches are urged to come forward if these tights sound familiar, and to check their drawers in case any of their tights may have sneaked out.

2

De-Cheesing

'Why do we have to de-cheese the shop *every morning*? We've been doing it *for weeks*,' Fluffanora said, plonking herself down next to the hundreds of Brew's witches who were flicking their fingers all over the shop. 'LET'S JUST ALL ADMIT THAT IT WILL ALWAYS SMELL OF CHEESE.'

'Strong spell, strong smell, we'll get it eventually,' Mrs Brew said patiently. 'Thank you for helping, too, Peggy.'

'Pleasure,' Peggy said, gagging.

'I can't believe that evil witch Miss Heks turned the shop into cheese during the good versus evil battle,' Fluffanora said, sniffing a pair of shoes. 'So unnecessary.'

Mrs Brew placed a feathery hat on a witch

mannequin. 'Well, it is a new era now. No more strange goings-on in Ritzy City. Nothing but normal life again, finally.'

'Excuse me, Mrs Brew, I found this outside,' one of her assistants said, handing her the *Silver Times* newspaper. 'I think we'd better check the tights, especially the lace ones.'

'Lavish tights … have robbed a gem shop,' Mrs Brew said.

Fluffanora cackled. 'Normal …'

Peggy straightened her shabby hat. 'We're working on that case. Oh, and I'd better go in a minute, I'm working on the old Sinkville Express railway, reconnecting the cities again! And it'll mean Tiga can visit easily.'

'Good,' Mrs Brew said. 'I don't like the thought of her trying to levitate all the way here, or riding her mum's rickety hoover.' She turned to Fluffanora. 'Could you scrape the cheese off the gloves over there, please.'

Fluffanora pretended not to hear her.

'Fluffanora!'

'Oh, all right,' she said, reluctantly. She held one up

and stared at it, wrinkling her nose in disgust. 'I miss Tiga. I bet she's having an absolutely sparkly time in Silver City …'

An extract from The Karens, *a very ~~terrifying~~ special book*

The strange thing about the Karens was NOT that there was a whole coven of them and they were all called Karen, OR that their cat was also called Karen, although that was admittedly weird. And let's not get started on their toes. No, the strange thing about the Karens was that they cared about only one thing. And that one thing was wishes.

Have you got a wish? Because if you do, the Karens might just come knocking …

Meet the stars of WITCH WARS

MEET **TIGA WHICABIM**

LIKES: Her slug

DISLIKES: Miss Heks's cheese water

FUN FACT: Her name is an anagram of 'I Am A Big Witch'

MEET **FRAN THE FABULOUS FAIRY**

LIKES: SHOW BUSINESS!

DISLIKES: People against glittery dust

FUN FACT: Her latest film won the award for Best and Only Fairy Film of The Year

MEET **PEGGY PIGWIGGLE**

LIKES: Adventures with Tiga

DISLIKES: People being mean

FUN FACT: Peggy, in an attempt to smooth her hair, once tried a spell designed for taming bears (because bear rhymes with hair ...)

MEET **FELICITY BAT**

LIKES: Levitating

DISLIKES: Anything not evil

FUN FACT: She is the granddaughter of
Celia Crayfish, the most evil
witch ever to rule Sinkville

MEET **AGGIE HOOF**

LIKES: Her best friend Fel-Fel (Felicity Bat)

DISLIKES: Anyone who doesn't follow
fashion trends

FUN FACT: Her pet is a diamond-studded
octopus

MEET **LIZZIE BEAST**

LIKES: Her best friend Patty Pigeon

DISLIKES: Being clumsy

FUN FACT: Her mother once sat on a
fairy and squashed her, kick-
starting The Fairy Riots

MEET **MILLY** AND **MOLLY**

LIKES: Milly and Molly

DISLIKES: Everyone else

FUN FACT: No one in Sinkville is exactly sure
who is Milly and who is Molly

MEET **FLUFFANORA BREW**

LIKES: Clutterbucks

DISLIKES: Silly contests like Witch Wars

FUN FACT: Fluffanora is actually called Anna,
but changed her name when she was
four years old on a whim

MEET **PATTY PIGEON**

LIKES: Quiet things

DISLIKES: Oh, nothing really, except maybe
chandeliers (since Witch Wars)

FUN FACT: She likes fun facts

Read the whole ritzy, glitzy, witchy series!